"You must have taken leave of your senses, Zach," Sarah replied.

"I'm obsessed with you. Are you here to tempt me?"

"I rather think it's the other way around."

"*I* tempt *you?* Why, Sarah, what a revelation. I had no idea."

Realizing her tactical mistake, Sarah retreated in denial. But Zach would have none of that. He took her hands, the softening around his mouth indulgent.

"How do I tempt you?" he asked, his tone smooth like silk.

"This conversation, for one," she said, summoning her most sanctimonious tone. "It is unseemly for a man and woman to speak so frankly."

He cocked his head. "Unseemly, huh? I certainly wouldn't want to be accused of that. Maybe we should let our bodies do the talking for us...."

Dear Reader,

There's so much in store for you this month from Silhouette Desire! First, don't miss *Cowboys Don't Cry* by Anne McAllister. Not only is this a *Man of the Month*— it's also the first book in her CODE OF THE WEST series. Look for the next two books in this series later in the year.

Another terrific miniseries, FROM HERE TO MATERNITY by Elizabeth Bevarly, also begins, with *A Dad Like Daniel*. These delightful stories about the joys of unexpected parenthood continue in April and June!

For those of you who like a touch of the otherworldly, take a look at Judith McWilliams's *Anything's Possible!* And the month is completed by Carol Devine's *A Man of the Land*, Audra Adams's *His Brother's Wife*, and *Truth or Dare* by Caroline Cross.

Next month, we celebrate the 75th *Man of the Month* with a very special Desire title, **That Burke Man** by **Diana Palmer.** It's part of her LONG, TALL TEXANS series, and I know you won't want to miss it!

Happy reading!

Lucia Macro
Senior Editor

Please address questions and book requests to:
Silhouette Reader Service
U.S.: 3010 Walden Ave., P.O. Box 1325, Buffalo, NY 14269
Canadian: P.O. Box 609, Fort Erie, Ont. L2A 5X3

CAROL
DEVINE
A MAN OF THE LAND

SILHOUETTE *Desire*®
Published by Silhouette Books
America's Publisher of Contemporary Romance

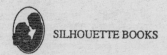

SILHOUETTE BOOKS

ISBN 0-373-05909-4

A MAN OF THE LAND

Printed in U.S.A.

Books by Carol Devine

Silhouette Desire

Beauty and the Beastmaster #816
A Man of the Land #909

CAROL DEVINE

lives in Colorado with her husband and three sons, including identical twins. When she's not playing pickup games of basketball and hunting for lost Reeboks, she's holed up in her office, dreaming of romantic heroes.

Her writing has won numerous awards, including the Romance Writers of America's 1992 Golden Heart for Short Contemporary Series Romance. She has also served as president of Rocky Mountain Fiction Writers. Readers may write to her at P.O. Box 9102, Englewood, CO 80111-9102

To Mom and Dad, with love

And to fellow writers Anita, Diane and Jessica
for all your advice and support

Prologue

———

Sarah Solomon hefted the poisoned beef in her hand and wondered if strychnine could be absorbed through human skin. If so, she'd pay with her life—a suitable penance considering the magnitude of the grievous sin she was about to commit. But if Butcher didn't die, she would.

Making sure she was downwind, she crept toward his shed. In the night quiet, the former chicken coop stood in a corner of the yard like a sentry with a slanted head. Above it curled a scrap of moon that cast few shadows. She'd chosen tonight for that reason.

Because of the bone-chilling cold, she wore every piece of clothing she owned—chemise, drawers and petticoat, two calico blouses, a sweater, her work skirt and Sunday best, even the gray wool gown from her mother's funeral. Although she wasn't allowed to wear gloves, she had a warm sheepskin coat. A stocking cap covered her bound-up hair.

Freezing mud sucked at the gaps in her knit wool stockings. Tonight, her first act of defiance had been to throw her clumsy wooden clogs into the fireplace. Not only would they slow her down, they'd leave a distinctive tread, one every member of the Community would recognize. First thing she'd do when she reached a town was find some comfortable shoes, maybe even a pair of those rubber-soled ones with wavy designs on the sides. She'd seen pictures of them in a magazine filched from the truck of the county's visiting nurse.

A cloud passed over the thin moon and she groped blindly for the shed. Rough weathered boards scraped her fingers. She followed her way around to the shed door, holding her breath the whole time. She needed to take Butcher by surprise. Once he heard her, all hell would break loose.

Butcher was the pride of Cal Solomon's life. He had bred the dog for trail sense and brute strength, crossing his best hound bitch with a pit bull he'd gotten from a pound in Great Falls. Once the puppies were born, Cal had picked the biggest male of the litter, shot the stud and drowned the remaining pups so Butcher would have no rivals, no peers.

A year later, the dog didn't. Broader in the head and chest than the hounds, Butcher could track with the best of them. But when it came time for the kill, he had no parallel. Sarah had seen the remains of coyotes he'd torn apart. She'd have little enough chance of escape with the hounds on her trail. She'd have none if Butcher was sicced on her.

In the dark silence, the clink of shifting chains drifted through the door. Vicious though he was, Sarah felt a stab of pity. She knew what it was like to be chained. She hadn't been privy to the rest of Cal's training methods because he'd worked the dog secretly—during renewal prayers—but she could well imagine what he'd done to make the tiny bundle of fur she'd cradled at birth turn into a ruthless killer. Maybe God would forgive this selfish act, for Butcher would be put out of his misery, too.

In one quick motion she yanked open the door and tossed the meat inside. Butcher barked, the sound wolfish and frenzied. Sarah darted around a corner and peered back at the main house, covering her ears because of the din. Sure enough, an uncertain flame from a match wavered from Cal's window. Then came a halo from a candle. The window flew open and Cal stuck his head outside, rifle in hand, his thick beard ruffling in the wind.

"Who's there?" he bellowed.

She froze, even though he couldn't see her, not crouched in the shadows. The slightest movement, however, would draw his attention. If he spotted something, he'd shoot now and ask questions later. Over the winter vandals had struck a number of other ranches in the Community. Cal had made his feelings clear then the same way he did now.

"Man's got a right to protect his own property!"

At the commanding sound of his master's voice, Butcher stopped barking. Metal clanked against wood. The dog snuffled along the baseboard and whined long and loud, puzzled, Sarah was sure, to smell somebody familiar. Cal must have heard because he swore.

"Damn dog," he muttered. "Waking me up for no reason."

The candle glow vanished. Sarah let out the breath she'd been holding. Butcher's chain dragged heavily, then silence. He'd found the meat. She bit her lip, remorse already eating away at her resolve. To keep from charging into the shed like an avenging angel, she dug her nails into her palm and told herself the pain was nothing compared to what the dog would inflict.

She made out the shadowy outline of the barn and headed there, stopping only to dip her bloodied hand into the horse trough. A thin coat of ice floated across the top, numbing her fingers. If only her conscience could be assuaged as easily.

The odor of manure from the cattle pens reached her, touched by the clean scent of budding trees. It reminded her of her purpose—to find a new life outside the Community. She spared a quick glance at the cabin. All quiet.

She smelled the barn before she reached it, a combination of musty hay, pungent horse, and well-fed cows, pleasant and familiar. Feeling for the latch, she pulled the door open enough to slip inside and closed it carefully because of the squeaky hinges. The absence of light was so great she couldn't make out the hand she held in front of her face. She used the stall wall on her right as a guide and whispered into the darkness.

"Twinkleberry?"

Sarah heard a nicker and a scrambling of hooves. The air stirred before a velvet nose butted her shoulder. She reached with her arms, her face already wet with tears, and hugged the gelding's thick neck.

"Goodbye," she said.

Planks creaked as more barn animals wakened. Sarah wound her arms around the other Percheron gelding, Old Brown. Then came the thinner neck of Nutkin, Cal's buckskin saddle horse. She considered taking him to ride, but Cal would launch a never-ending pursuit if she stole something as valuable as his horse. Besides, she hadn't ridden in some eight years, ever since her mother had married Cal and he'd become her stepfather.

At the rear of the barn she found the ladder leading to the hayloft. Climbing the first four rungs, she stretched and felt under the straw heaped on the second floor. Her fist closed around a cotton bundle. She wrapped the loose top of it— once a pillowcase—around her hand and let it drop. The makeshift sack clunked heavily against the ladder as she descended.

She jumped to the floor and plunged her hand inside. Pushing past her lighter provisions, she felt for the heavy metal cylinder that lay at the bottom. She'd uncovered the flashlight a week ago under a loosened brick while cleaning the main hearth. After examining the long chrome tube and unblinking glass eye, she'd managed to turn it on and immediately realized what power she'd held. Light without fuel. She wouldn't have to carry candles or an oil lamp. The flashlight would make all the difference in her escape.

To Sarah, it was a sign from God.

The squeak of the barn door brought her head up sharply. A man's silhouette stood at the threshold of the barn, backed by the ruddy light of a coal oil lantern. She heard the rachet sound of a rifle being cocked.

"Lessen you want to die," Cal said, "show yourself."

Sarah shrank back and cast the sack behind her, searching for the rear door of the barn. At best, she had only a few seconds to find a way out. Her spine flattened against the wall. She gripped the sack in one hand and spread the other one out, despair blinding her more than the dark. Even if she found the door, it led into the cattle pens, occupied at this time of year by heifers and newborn calves. She'd risk losing a few toes going out there in her stocking feet.

Cal shoved the door aside with his hip, opening it fully. Reflected flame reddened the oily skin above his beard and blotted out his eyes, making holes in his wide face. His denim overalls were snapped on one side, exposing the red buttoned front of his faded union suit. He paced forward, sending shadows leaping along the walls. The horses shifted nervously.

Too late to hide. Holding the sack behind her skirt, Sarah stepped from the shadows. "Hello, Cal."

"What the hell you be doing out here?"

"Heard Butcher barking," she said, lapsing into the colloquial English used by most people of the Community. The tactic had saved her a beating more than once. "Thought I'd best see what got him all riled up. Ain't found nothing, though."

"You check the outhouse?"

"First thing I done. Empty as a corncrib in August. I thought to check the cattle pens next. Them newborns sure make easy pickings." She turned, trying to keep the look of her arms natural as she kept the pillowcase hidden at her side.

"Nope," Cal said, catching her arm. "You git back to the house. Ain't right for a woman to be out wandering around in the middle of the night."

Sarah nodded, afraid the sudden hope she felt might be betrayed in her voice. If Cal stayed behind, that would give her the few minutes she needed to run to the south pasture. She'd spent an hour crisscrossing it yesterday, laying down many trails of her scent. Fording the river would give her extra insurance once Cal discovered her gone and released the hounds. With luck and the cover of darkness, she'd make it to the highway by daybreak.

She scooted by him and made it outside. He'd set a lantern in the middle of the yard between the house and barn. Disturbing it would alert him immediately, so she left it there, letting it illuminate her way as she quickened her steps. The only thing between her and freedom was Butcher's shed. When she got near it, she began to run.

A fierce barking tailed into the wind, the likes of which she'd thought to never hear again. Sarah staggered in disbelief. Butcher.

The pillowcase slipped from her hands and cartwheeled to the ground, spilling the contents. She dropped to her knees, grabbing matches, lye soap, a sack of beans. Above the sound of barking, she heard Cal bellow.

"Sarah!"

She looked up and froze. He'd come out of the barn and was advancing on her, rifle in hand, his eyes taking in the scatter of provisions littering the ground. She knew the exact moment he spotted the flashlight. A look of murderous rage changed his face.

Sarah jumped and ran. The crack of a rifle ripped the air. She zigzagged and Butcher's incessant baying covered her crash against the shed. Beyond terror, she hunkered down and clutched dirt, searching for a stick, a rock, anything.

Suddenly the collar of her coat was grabbed. Cal picked her up bodily and slammed her against the wall. Splinters bit into her cheek. Sarah gritted her teeth to keep from whimpering. If nothing else, she was through whimpering.

He barked a short guttural command to Butcher and the dog stopped howling. Then he grabbed her shoulder and turned her around. "Did you really think you could get away from me?"

Sarah didn't answer. She was through answering, too.

"Got a beau waiting out here, don't you?"

She raised her chin at the familiar accusation.

He prodded her with the rifle. "Answer me!"

"There's no beau. You never let me stop working long enough to find one."

His blow to her head sent her spinning across the yard. She sprawled in the icy mud. Something long and hard pressed into her belly. The flashlight. She reached for it, gathering courage and, God forbid, resolve. He'd killed her mother's spirit. She wasn't going to let him kill hers.

He stomped over to her. She curled into a ball, making herself a smaller target, and watched his feet, readying herself. He drew his leg back and she turned enough to take the kick in the belly, where it was better absorbed by her clothes.

Reaching up, she hooked an arm around his leg. Grunting in surprise, he lashed out with the butt of the rifle but her intention had not been to throw off his balance. Instead she used his leg for leverage and rammed the flashlight directly into his groin.

He screamed and bent over double, clawing at her hand. She drew the flashlight back, bringing it forward in an arc. It smashed into the side of his head, shattering the flashlight's plastic cover. Cal fell forward, landing on top of her. With a shudder, she squirmed out from underneath him.

Sarah scrambled up, the broken flashlight held at the ready, and paused, her gasps fogging in the cold air. He didn't move. She snatched up the rifle, her other arm still wound up to swing again, afraid he would somehow spring to life.

Blood trickled from a bruise growing on the side of his head and she realized he wouldn't be coming after her any time soon. She backed up and her feet tripped over something solid. Balancing the gun in the crook of her arm, she scooped up her sack of beans and the soap, dropping them it into the pillowcase. Swiftly, she gathered the rest of her provisions. She had to get moving. Time was a'wasting.

She used rope from the barn to tie Cal's hands and feet, then hefted the rifle. It was heavy, too heavy to carry. Besides, she had no ammunition and wasn't about to spare the time to go back to the cabin to search for some. She glanced at Butcher's shed and realized what she had to do. Once Cal came to his senses, he'd come after her with a vengeance. And he'd use Butcher to do it.

With the tip of the gun barrel, Sarah pushed open the shed door. A low growl caused the hairs at the back of her neck to stand on end. She aimed toward the sound before shifting sideways to let light in from the lantern outside. The glow was enough to pick up the shine of raw meat lying untouched on the dirt floor and the gleam of canine teeth, clenched in a snarl. Above the white fangs glowered eyes red with warning.

Sarah blanched. She hadn't seen him this close in eleven months' time, since she'd had charge of the whelping pen. If it wasn't for the short length of chain that linked his leather collar to a bolt sticking out of the ground, her throat would undoubtedly have been torn out by now.

Keeping the gun aimed in his direction, she inched her foot out and nudged the meat closer to him. He stopped growling and licked his chops, focusing on the meat. Saliva dripped from his glistening jowls.

"Eat," she commanded.

He looked up at her and actually wagged his stub of a tail. But he didn't eat.

"What do I have to do? Feed you myself?"

He sniffed the air between them and his muzzle wrinkled, showing scars from numerous fights. Careful to keep a good grip on the gun, she picked up the meat with her other hand and held it out.

"Come on, boy. Come and get it."

Butcher regarded her with interest, but it didn't appear to be culinary. He sat back on his haunches and cocked his head, chastened but alert, the pose of a good dog. Except Sarah knew he was far from that.

"Last chance," she said, and tossed the meat between his front paws.

He stayed like a statue, his gaze fastened on her, his flanks quivering with tension, showing every rib. Why wouldn't he eat? He was obviously starving. Just looking at him brought tears to her eyes. She scrubbed at them, furious at her foolishness, for her future depended on destroying him. The gun was loaded. All she had to do was pull the trigger. It would be easy to kill him. He was chained. He couldn't run, couldn't hide.

Neither could she.

Very slowly, Sarah knelt. Using one of the filthy rags from his bedding, she scooped up the meat and then laid the gun on the floor. She couldn't kill, not face-to-face, in cold blood.

With a shiver, she tossed the meat into a bucket of scum in the corner of the shed. Butcher pricked his ears at the plopping sound, so far out of reach. She gazed at him, feeling her heart pound in her throat.

"Didn't he even leave you any water?" she asked. Her voice broke. "Butch?"

His head came down and his body curled in a queer wiggle. He moved forward, belly low, and wiggled harder, sending a clear message. Scarcely believing, Sarah backed up a step. He came to the end of his chain and tried to roll over, but there wasn't enough room. He curled on his side and eyed her, tail thumping.

She extended her hand. He pawed the air and tipped up his heavy jaw, exposing his throat. She came forward and bent down, barely in reach. His cold, wet nose met her fingers. Frightened, she jerked her hand back.

He wheezed, straining forward against the chain closing around his throat. With a shaky thumb, she touched the top of his head, and stroked it once, twice. His tail thumped harder.

Sarah crept closer so he wouldn't have to strain himself and petted his furrowed brow with her whole hand, then scratched his ears in the way he used to love. He still loved it. Shuddering in ecstasy, he whimpered.

"Butcher?" she asked. "Do you really remember?"

He yelped, the sound at once both happy and mournful. Swallowing back the lump in her throat, Sarah reached for his collar. He leapt to his feet, trembling with anticipation.

"I'm letting you free. If you come with me, I can't promise a steady supply of food," she told him. "But I can promise you won't be chained up anymore. And you'll always have fresh water."

She drew the heavy link chain away and he streaked by her out the door. Sarah chucked the rifle beneath his bedding and followed.

Outside, the wind rushed through the trees, making a cackling noise. Just underneath, she heard a more insidious sound. She turned, searching in the lantern light. Butcher was licking the blood from Cal's slack face.

Squaring her shoulders, she gathered up what was left of her provisions and plunged across the field. Butcher could come or go as he pleased. What mattered was her journey. It had begun. She would find her own place in the world.

A belonging place.

One

Zach Masterson didn't like the sight that greeted him when he stepped outside the trailer. Last night when he'd arrived at the Bar M, it had been too dark to see much more than an outline of the various ranch buildings. Now, in the full light of day, Zach spent a moment studying exactly what he'd missed.

Junk littered the yard. Most of it was farm machinery, pieces of tractors, combines, even the rusting hood from an old Chevy pickup. Whole sections of the corral next to the main barn were missing, and the barbed wire fence along the lane leading to the road sagged like the back of an old mule. The tack shed looked ready to collapse, while the little two-stall barn where his mother used to keep a milk cow already had. Obviously there hadn't been money spent on capital improvements to the ranch in years.

He veered left and came to a stop beneath one of the cottonwoods that ringed the yard. The main house still stood, rising in all its two-story glory. It was easily in the best shape of all the ranch buildings, despite the boarded-up windows and peeling paint.

Zach wished he had bulldozed it ten years ago when his father had died and he'd had the chance.

He pivoted on his heel and headed toward the barn, stirring puffs of dust with every step he took. His mind skipped ahead to all he'd have to accomplish over the next few weeks. Before arriving at the Bar M, he'd been certain he could make short work of selling the place. The Masterson ranch was famous for its spring-fed pastures, a rarity in semi-arid Colorado. Once the hay fields were harvested and the cattle rounded up and sold, getting rid of everything else figured to be a cinch. But no one in their right mind would buy the place as is.

He paused next to the old corn silo pocked with rust and calculated how much it would cost to fix things up, both in time and money. He'd told his partner, Manuelo, he'd only be away from their business, Amazon Exploration Guides, for a few days, two weeks at most. If he ended up staying here longer than that, he'd lose money, not to mention his sanity. Already he missed Rio Negro and the cover of broad green leaves, of shade so deep it felt like night, of the constant hum of jungle life. Here, the blinding sun bothered him, used as he was to its heat. Everything was so open in Colorado, so brown and dry and exposed.

Zach heard voices and changed direction. He could stand anything if it had a foreseeable end. He would make sure it took no more than a month to get the ranch in shape and sold. Jackson, the ranch foreman, was a goner for letting things get this bad. With the cooperation of the rest of the Bar M ranch hands, he would get out of here by the end of October. Tops.

Zach reached the fence and acknowledged the four men gathered there with a brisk nod. His motives would be suspect if he appeared too friendly. Three of them had never set eyes on him before, and Ty Coburn, the old-timer of the bunch, hadn't seen Zach show his stuff since he'd left the ranch for good thirteen years ago.

Coburn looked him over, a yellow, tobacco-stained grin on his lean and leathery face. These days, more silver than gold threaded the droopy mustache. "Pretty fancy duds you got on there, boss."

Zach didn't bother to glance down at his olive T-shirt and camouflage fatigues, scrounged years ago from an army surplus store. The only concession he'd made to the cattle country uniform was his lizard-skin cowboy boots, bought on the way in from the airport last night. The Vibram soles of his jungle boots were too thick to fit into a stirrup. "Don't I pass inspection?"

"You're missing something."

"And what might that be?"

Ty flicked the brim of his battered Stetson hat. "Can't be a self-respecting cattleman without a hat."

"I'll never be a cattleman, self-respecting or otherwise." Simply because he needed their cooperation didn't mean he should give them a false impression about why he was here.

"How about a cowboy?"

Zach squinted into the sun, appearing to consider the question. He knew the word *cowboy,* overused by the urban population, was a derogatory term to these men. Deadpan, he said, "Not since I was knee-high to a grasshopper."

Ty shook his head. "You haven't changed much, by the sound of it. Still poking fun at what you should hold most dear."

"What's that—grasshoppers?"

Two of the hands actually cracked a smile. Zach used the moment to study all four faces, shaded by the ever-present hats. These men were tough and range-hardened, and at this particular moment he hadn't earned the respect of any of them, despite the appreciation they might show for his wit. Respect went out the window when a man's job was at stake.

"Jackson tell any of you why I've come back to the Bar M?"

"Nope. Been lots of rumors, though," Ty replied evenly.

The other three men stopped chuckling and the feeling of camaraderie abruptly ended.

"My family has decided to sell the ranch," Zach said bluntly, addressing the entire group. "Any questions?"

He expected the sullen silence that followed and let it build while he pulled on a pair of roping gloves, eyeing each man in turn. No point in pulling punches, not when he was talking about their future. "This ranch hasn't been home to anyone in the Masterson family for a long time. That's why we're selling."

"What about Bram?" Ty asked. "Not long ago he told me as the eldest son, he'd make sure the Bar M never got sold."

"Bram's married now, with a child on the way. He and his wife have their own place up the road, and other things to worry about besides the running of the Bar M. You may as well know—no one else wants to hold on to it. Bram was overruled."

"Four to one?" Ty asked, making reference to all five Masterson siblings.

Zach nodded. "I've been lobbying for this the longest, so I got elected to oversee the sale."

"What about us? How soon will you be laying us off?"

The question came from one of the ranch hands. From Ty's description during the ride in from the airport, Zach recalled his name as Jason Miller. Beneath the straw brim, his peppered hair was trimmed and his jaw closely shaven. Even before Zach checked out the ring finger of his left hand, he guessed what Miller's problem was. Job security was number one when a man had a family to support.

"You'll be paid through the time of sale, plus two weeks severance," Zach said. "Beyond that, I won't make any guarantees. Whoever buys this place gets to decide who leaves and who stays on."

He studied the rugged faces, looking for telltale signs of resentment. Better to nip such feelings in the bud rather than let them fester. He'd led various kinds of expeditions for years and learned that truth was best, especially if you wanted your crew to work hard without complaint.

"I mean to get top dollar for this place. Right now, it needs some major fixing up, which means hard work and long hours for each of you. If you want to quit and draw your wages now, I'll understand. But if you stay, I expect you to see the job through until the ranch is sold." He looked directly at Ty. "You staying, Coburn?"

"Reckon I will, boss."

"As of today, you're now the ranch foreman. If Jackson gives you a hard time, tell him not to bother cashing this week's paycheck. It won't be good."

"Right, boss."

Zach shifted his attention to the next order of business and scanned the dozen horses in the corral. He didn't plan to ride long, just hard, seeking something from speed that he hadn't been able to find anywhere else since he'd gotten here.

He chose a buckskin mare, the best of the lot brought down from summer pasture. Coburn mentioned she hadn't been ridden all season, which only served to make her more attractive. In spite of her being rank, fifteen minutes later he had her roped, brushed, bridled and saddled.

"Like you never left," said Coburn, shaking his head.

"Some things you don't forget." Zach grabbed the reins and a good hunk of black mane. The buckskin quivered all over. "At least, I hope so."

Coburn went to her head, holding the bridle, while Zach mounted. "You sure about this, now? You can let one of these other young bucks have a go at her first. She's green and mean."

"Open the gate," said Zach. "If she has the room, she'll run."

The buckskin took off at a dead gallop, which suited him just fine. He gave her her head, and she headed west. The land stretched in ever-rising hills, each one higher than the one before it. Once, all of them had been part of the Masterson range. Soon, none of them would be.

Abruptly, he jerked the reins and steered the buckskin sideways, cutting upward to the top of the nearest ridge. The mare obeyed without protest, though Zach sensed she was prone to shy if he should suddenly decide to change direction.

Once he topped the ridge, the wind blowing in his face held a trace of burning wood. Piñon, he guessed, judging from the tang. Unexplained fires were always reason for concern. He scanned the shallow valley on the other side. The land was rocky, cut by wind and the remnants of what had once been a good-size river. Now all that remained was a ribbon of water that snaked its way along the bottom of the shallow valley.

The creek was a magnet for all types of creatures, including people. Zach had a hunch some itinerant hikers had set up house, complete with campfire. His jaw tightened. Trespassing on private land was inexcusable, especially when there were so many public hiking trails on the federal preserve west of the ranch's border.

A wisp of rising smoke led his eye to a grove of golden-leafed cottonwoods. He spurred the buckskin into a slow ascent, careful of his approach. At the bottom, he steered the horse into the creek to mask the sound of plodding hooves. Poachers were always a possibility. He wanted to be absolutely sure of what he was getting into before he rode in.

This time of year the creek ran low and fast, fueled by early snow in the mountains to the west and the steep slope of the ridge. Cottonwoods, willows, and scrub oak grew on either side of the water, screening what lay ahead. He rounded a bend and spotted a flash of solid white, unnatural against the shifting view of trees and water. Zach reined back, taking shelter under the shade of a giant willow overhanging the bank.

Whoever it was, she faced away from him. At least, he thought the slight figure belonged to a she. Behind her, sunshine sparkled on the fast-moving water. Dressed in something long, white and flowing, the full extent of her build was hidden by wavy brown hair that fell past her hips. Girl or woman? She was fairly tall, but with her back to him, it was hard to tell for sure.

She waded into the creek and the current took the hem of her petticoat, sending it in a swirl around her legs. The undertow must have been strong, for she swayed and held out her arms for balance. Her hair swung like a curtain over one shoulder, revealing a gap between her petticoat and her chemise. Her waist was narrow and well-defined. Delicate hollows marked her spine. Hips flared into subtly provocative curves.

Woman. Definitely a woman.

Poised like a dragonfly above the water, she stepped cautiously, intent with purpose. Zach squinted, trying to figure out what she was doing. Fishing? If so, she should be wearing pants and waders. This late in September, the water would be freezing.

He steered the buckskin to the very edge of the concealing shade, closing the distance to twenty feet. If she turned, she would see him, but it was a gamble he was willing to take.

She reached a waist-high boulder in the middle of the creek and placed a hand on top, using it for support. Against the speckled granite, he saw that she clutched a gnarled brown root. She stooped and fished a good-size stone up from the creek bottom, then dunked the root before laying it out on the boulder and pounding it with the stone. White suds began to appear.

Zach sniffed the shifting breeze. Clean. When mixed with water, mashed yucca root had a fresh scent and made a pretty good soap. He himself had used it in a pinch.

She bent forward from the waist and splashed upward with her hands, drenching both her hair and the front of her petticoat. Sunlight angled through the sodden fabric, revealing the outline of long, slender legs. Straightening, she gathered suds from the boulder and dumped them on her head. The froth of white raced down her hair. Flexing her hands, she worked the lather in and tilted back to bask her face in the sun. Her neat profile angled into a lovely neck, supple and strong. Remnants of foam dripped down her chemise, molding it to her body.

Zach studied the willowy torso with an appreciative eye. The fluid arms, the elegant points of her shoulders, the athletic extension of a body honed and fit drew him like nothing else could. His first lover had been a ballet dancer and this woman had the same nimble deftness that came with extreme discipline. A rock climber, maybe, come down from the foothills?

She bent forward to rinse, efficient with grace. He wished she'd remove her clothes. They were superfluous given this remote setting. And judging by how wet she was already, it would make her life easier, not to mention his. Just the thought of seeing her naked made him unbearably hard. Sitting astride didn't help. Neither did the buckskin. When he shifted in the saddle, she shied and danced forward.

Sarah heard the rapid pattern of skipping hooves, coming fast. Dear God, she thought in panic. Cal had finally found her.

She straightened like a shot. Her hair sailed through the air, spraying droplets in a high, flying arc. The buckskin neighed in fear and reared in the face of this new threat. Thrown forward, Zach jerked the reins short, keeping the horse's head up so she wouldn't buck.

Terrified, Sarah raised her hands to ward off a blow. How like Cal to ambush her in broad daylight, when she'd least expect it.

Staggering, her bare feet floundered on the rocky creek bed. Her arms pinwheeled and she lost her balance, landing hard on her backside. The breath went clean out of her. She heard the thrashing grunt of a frightened horse and a man's voice, low and calm.

"Whoa, girl. Easy."

Sarah sat up and shook the hair from her eyes. The wild-eyed horse was tan in color, with black markings, just like Nutkin. But larger. Much larger. And the man on top did not look familiar in the least.

She rose slowly, noting the expert way he settled his mount. He hooked the frightened horse into a neat circle under a tight, uncompromising rein, showing off the bronzed biceps of an experienced wrangler. Horse and rider halted a few feet away.

"You okay?" he asked.

Still breathless, Sarah didn't answer. He sat his horse easy, with his hands relaxed and his stomach concave in that deceptive slouch all expert cowboys employed. Yet he was without the wide-brimmed hat she'd come to expect. Black, shaggy hair brushed a jaw shadowed with whisker stubble. Olive-green cotton stretched tight across the front of his broad chest. Called a T-shirt because of its distinctive shape, Sarah decided that on this man, the shirt was a clear V, for while his shoulders were wide, the rest of him tapered into a cougar-like leanness. Instead of blue jeans, which in her experience was the attire of choice for most men in cattle country, he wore trousers splotched with earthen colors— black, green and tan. Most surprising of all, his pointy-toed boots looked brand-spanking new.

Sarah wrung out the hem of her petticoat, eyeing him warily. In spite of his unusual clothing, he had the face of a cowboy—sun-browned, rugged, and inordinately appealing.

"You always sneak up on a body like that?" she asked.

The crow's feet around his blue eyes crinkled in amusement. "Only ones like yours."

Sarah had heard enough ribald comments in the past few months to recognize a come-on when she heard one. Oddly disappointed, she raised her chin a notch.

He dropped his reins and placed both hands upon his heart in mock pain. "If looks could kill. Hey, I didn't mean to offend you. Give me a smile and tell me I'm forgiven."

Charmed by his rueful manner, Sarah hesitated, drawn in despite her better judgment. There was an air of offhand authority about him that invited trust. This was a man of the land, tested by the rigors of sun and wind. She could see it in the confident way he held himself. Yet she would do well to remain wary, for the newspapers were full of sinister stories of what happened when trust was given too easily. Besides, he definitely had the look of a renegade about him. It was in his clothes and the unruly hair, and especially, the hunger in his eyes when he looked at her.

"I'm really not such a bad guy once you get to know me. How about I help you out of there and we start over?" Zach extended a hand.

She took a stiff step backward, which wasn't exactly the response Zach had been looking for, and shaded her face against the glare of the sun. Her eyes were the deep brown of old pennies, large and arresting, especially when surrounded by a thick fringe of black lashes made spiky by the water. In contrast, her complexion was fine, like smooth, sand-colored clay. There was no makeup that he could see, just the last sunburn of the season.

Zach reined in the buckskin with one hand while doing his best to maintain his Gene Autry imitation with the other. She didn't seem to be buying it, though. Retreating, she stepped onto the bank without taking her eyes off him. Suspicious little thing, wasn't she?

When she reached dry ground, she combed her fingers through her wet hair, holding it away from her shoulder to keep the heavy mass from dripping on her clothes. The attempt was in vain. The material of her chemise was saturated, clearly delineating her high, rounded breasts. The water must have been cold, for her erect nipples showed through the flimsy fabric.

He couldn't help but smile. Maybe she was right to be suspicious of him. He was not a man adverse to taking what was freely offered, *free* being the operative word. Time for his most original line. "My name is Zach Masterson. What's yours?"

She shook her head. Her refusal to answer irritated him, especially since her teeth were chattering. Well, hell, he thought. There was more than one way to communicate. He wrapped the reins around the saddlehorn, pulled his shirt over his head and offered it to her with a grand flourish. "Even if I don't know your name, I can't resist a damsel in distress."

Appalled at his boldness, Sarah's gaze traveled up his corded arm to the sinewy muscles of his chest. Most cowboys had tans that ended at the necks and sleeves of their snap-buttoned shirts. He was deeply tanned all over, a sight she'd rarely seen in the flesh. Certainly, she'd never seen it this close.

"Don't stand there with your mouth open. Take it," he urged, dangling the shirt in front of her nose.

Her mouth had indeed been open. Sarah snapped it shut and felt the red creep up her cheeks. Worse, there were other physical manifestations of her flustered feelings. Not only was she blushing, her stomach felt queer, like she'd swallowed half a dozen butterflies.

"Come on. No cooties, I promise. I can't let you stand there shivering. You're practically naked."

"N-naked?" she sputtered.

"She speaks. I was beginning to wonder if I'd been hearing things and had a deaf-mute on my hands."

"I'm hardly naked," she announced, and planted her hands on her hips, amazed at his audacity. Did he think her so brazen as to wash in full daylight without a stitch on?

"The face of an angel, the body of Venus and the voice of a siren. Can you sing, too?" he asked, taking one last stab at winning a smile from her.

Sarah glanced down at herself, wondering if he was making fun of her. It wouldn't be the first time since she'd left the Community that someone had commented on her clothes. Her chemise lay plastered to her skin, revealing every outline of her breasts and belly. Mortified, she frantically arranged her hair in front to cover herself.

"You need something a little more substantial than that. Not that I'm complaining or anything, but I figured the least I could do is offer you the shirt off my back." Grinning, he tossed his shirt at her.

On reflex, Sarah caught it. Remnants of his body heat warmed her fingers. Even his scent reached her, earthy and male. She dropped the shirt as though burned, and crossed her arms over her chest, effectively shielding her breasts. "Stop gawking at me!"

"If you don't want me to stare, put on some clothes."

"I'll have you know, these are my clothes."

"Oh, really?" His gaze raked over her in a most insulting way.

"Unmentionables maybe, but clothes all the same."

"Unmentionables?"

"Perfectly decent unmentionables," she said, biting off each word. "They certainly cover more than most getups I've seen lately."

Zach was struck by her old-fashioned choice of words. She also had a slight accent, one he couldn't place. That was unusual, for he'd traveled all over the world and could speak a smattering of phrases in a dozen different languages. "That accent ... is it German?"

Stunned by the accuracy of his perception, Sarah could only blink in surprise. Some founders of the Community, her mother among them, had been Mennonites, descended from German immigrants. Pennsylvania Dutch had been a second language in the home of her youth.

"You don't look German. Not with those dark eyes and hair."

"I have some Native American blood."

"American Native Indian?"

"Crow. On my father's side," she said, wondering why she'd admitted that much. Ever since she'd run away, she'd been very circumspect about telling anyone about her background. Shivering anew, she turned her back and hurriedly tugged wet material away from her skin.

"The view's not bad from here, either," he said, laughter underpinning his voice.

"If you possessed a speck of decency, you'd turn 'round, yourself," Sarah flung over her shoulder.

"And miss the show?"

"And to think I thought you were a gentleman."

"I sacrificed my shirt, didn't I? Don't you recognize a chivalrous gesture when you see one?"

"A true gentleman does not make sport of another's choice in clothing. Nor would he sneak up on a lady while she's washing her hair."

"He might feel justified if the lady was on his land."

"Rest assured, I'll be off it by nightfall."

Shoulders rigid, she leapt to higher ground, snagged a blanket laid out on the grass and flung it around her shoulders. Several articles of clothing were draped over the chokecherry bushes that grew along the bank. There were a couple of long-sleeved blouses, a full-length skirt, and a heavy-looking gray dress. The impractical style of the clothes bothered him. Only a fool would wear such things on a camping trip.

"Laundry day?" he asked.

Clutching the blanket like a shawl, she marched to a propylene tarp spread out nearby. The hem of her petticoat trailed the ground in uneven tatters, and the edges of the blanket were ragged from use. Wiping her bare feet, she slid them into a battered pair of Nike sneakers, complete with wave logo. The shoes had seen better days. The laces were frayed and the tongues hung out, looking incongruous next to her trim ankles. She wore no socks.

Could she be a runaway? From experience, Zach recognized the signs of both poverty and pride. But judging from her speech, she was highly educated. He recalled the taut curves of her body hidden by the blanket. And he was willing to bet she was well over the age of consent.

Zach checked the clearing behind her, looking for evidence of a boyfriend. Maybe that would explain the chilly reception he was receiving. Certainly she wouldn't be out here by herself.

The area had been cleared of brush, but there was little in the way of equipment. He didn't see a tent or sleeping bags, although a pack hung from a low cottonwood branch. The pack's bottom looked to be reinforced with stiff leather. Primitive laces crisscrossed the sides, attaching a smooth type of fabric that was too limp to be Gore-Tex water-repellent fabric, nylon, or even canvas. It was hardly big enough to carry ten pounds of gear, much less enough food for two.

Next to the pack were several bunches of dried greens, tied upside down. A plastic water jug was also strung up. Underneath, stacked deadwood partially covered by a garbage bag indicated she planned to stay awhile, although he couldn't imagine why. She had no shelter.

"Are you lost?" he asked.

She made a noise that sounded suspiciously like a snort, and headed toward a small campfire. Surrounded by fist-size rocks, it was covered by a blackened grate. A varied collection of tin cans sat on top, wisping steam. Whatever was simmering smelled of sage.

"What's cooking?" he asked, trying a more innocuous subject.

She rubbed the wet ends of her hair smartly between the two sides of the blanket. Zach raised an eyebrow at the continued silent treatment and spurred the buckskin up the bank, halting short of the tarp where she'd taken refuge. The corners were held down by a small black Bible and a thick paperback dictionary. Not exactly your regular campsite reading material. Other personal items were arranged in a neat row along one side. She didn't have much. Toothpaste, toothbrush, comb, eating utensils, a straw hat held down by a pocketknife on the ragged brim, and matches.

"I asked you a question," he said.

The blanket snapped, emphasizing the silence.

"Then it must be you who smells good enough to eat."

She glared at him. He returned the look, wondering what else he could do to break the ice. She secured the blanket by knotting it around her shoulders, and picked up the comb. Zach considered his options as she worked the tangles from her hair, sorting through various gambits designed to get a rise out of her. He settled on the most obvious.

"Where's your boyfriend?"

Her hands stilled.

"He won't like finding me here, will he? Not that I can blame him."

Her gaze went directly to his. "Who are you talking about?"

"You know. The guy you're camping with."

He said it in the most casual way possible but her reaction still surprised him. She stopped fooling with her hair and shoved all her belongings into the middle of the tarp, gathering it up.

"Was it something I said?"

"I must go."

"What happened?" Zach asked, shifting to dismount. "You two have a fight or something?"

In a flash, she dropped her things and clutched his leg, forcing him to stay in the saddle. Startled, the buckskin jerked sideways. Zach put pressure on the reins without taking his eyes off the woman's pale face. Whoever this guy was, he had her good and scared.

"Don't leave your horse," she said. "He will be even angrier if he finds you here." She glanced over her shoulder, searching among the trees. "Where did you see him?"

He reached down and gripped her chin, forcing her to look at him. "Did he hurt you?"

She let go of his leg, resisting the contact. "Psalms 17:13. 'Deliver me from the wicked by thy sword, from men by thy hand, O'Lord, from men whose portion in life is of the world.'"

Zach was unfamiliar with the biblical reference. When he was a kid, he'd managed to get kicked out of every school he'd been in, including Sunday school. He kept his gaze steady, studying the defiance in her dark eyes. "Not all men are wicked. No one deserves to be hurt, especially at the hand of another."

She went still. "My worldly father used to say the same thing."

"Your father was a wise man. Did he give you a name?"

After a long pause, she nodded. "Sarah."

"Sarah what?"

"Sarah...Smith."

Zach filed the pause between her last name and first for future reference. Sarah was not an especially good liar. He let her go, but extended his hand in clear welcome, the tips of his fingers nearly touching her face. "You look pretty clean to me, Sarah."

He kept his expression carefully neutral, allowing her to come to a decision in her own good time. After what seemed like a year, her hand snaked out from the blanket. At least she had knowledge of the most rudimentary of social skills. He was beginning to wonder.

"Pleased to meet you, Zacharias," she said gravely.

"It's Zach."

"Zach," she repeated, inclining her head.

"Sarah," he said, savoring the sound. It reminded him of a spring breeze, fresh with promise. He pressed the rough callus on her palm but resisted the urge to investigate, vowing to save that for later. And there would be a later. She was both a mystery and a challenge, his two favorite pursuits in life.

"So who's this guy you're so afraid of?" he asked.

"You mustn't concern yourself. I'll be off your land by nightfall, I promise you."

"When I rode in, I could see for miles. I didn't see anyone here but you."

"You said you saw him."

"Did I? I thought I simply asked about your boyfriend."

"Oh. Well, as you can see, I am a woman alone."

She said it baldly, a statement of fact, and again he wondered at her odd way of putting things.

She stroked the buckskin's shoulder. "She reminds me of another horse I know. What's her name?"

"What's the name of the other horse?"

"Nutkin."

"Nutkin it is, then."

She smiled for the first time. Two of her front teeth were slightly crooked. The small imperfection only heightened her appeal. He despised artifice and hadn't met a woman yet who didn't practice it in some form. Maybe the lovely Sarah would prove the exception.

Sure of his welcome, he withdrew his boot from the stirrup and swung his leg over the saddle. In his concentration, he didn't see the streak of brown hurtling from the screen of trees in front of him. But he heard Sarah's yell and felt the buckskin lurch as the dog attacked.

"No, Butcher!"

The buckskin reared, squealing in surprise and pain. Off balance, Zach fell across the saddle. The reins snaked from his hands and struck the frightened horse in the face, sending her into a spin. Zach grabbed her mane, fighting to regain his seat. He barely managed.

Butcher was a dog—a howling, snapping, angry dog. He barked and darted like a dervish. The buckskin bolted into the creek, kicking up water, scaring herself even more. Zach hung on, but the dog never let up. Barking madly, it lunged around the horse's hocks like a dangerous bee, driving her wild.

From the corner of his eye, Zach saw Sarah toss the blanket off her shoulders, then splash into the water after them, shouting and waving her arms. He spurred the buckskin away from her, yelling for her to stay clear.

The buckskin took exception and twisted high, throwing him off. He somersaulted through the air. The surface of the water rippled, glinting the rays of the sun. He threw out his hands.

The last thing Zach saw was rocks. Lots of rocks.

Two

Sarah splashed into the creek, caught Butcher's collar and yanked him back from the flailing hooves. She heard Zach shout, and hauled the dog sideways, terrified of getting trampled. Her shoes came off, swept away by the swift current, and her petticoat billowed. The horse must not have liked that, either, because it flew by, kicking out with its hind legs. Sarah ducked just in time.

She heard a huge splash and the horse galloped past her, wheeled and scrambled up the far side of the creek, riderless. Whipping her head around, she spotted Zach. He had landed facedown where many jagged rocks broke the surface of the shallow water.

"Oh, dear God."

Ordering Butcher to heel, she rushed downstream, dropped to her knees and flipped Zach over. Bright blood gushed down his face, pulsing from somewhere near the top of his head. She tore off her chemise and wiped his brow, searching for the wound. It was high across his forehead, just under the hairline. A jagged tear, a good three inches long, had ripped his scalp to the bone. The creek ran so fast it threatened to wash over him, making his stillness all the more frightening.

Sarah propped his head out of the water and forced the edges of the wound closed with her fingers. With her other hand, she dunked the chemise and wrung it over his face.

"Zach?"

Blood and mud washed away, but his eyes remained closed. Against his pale jaw, his day's growth of beard stood out starkly.

"Wake up," she prodded, shaking him.

Not so much as an eyelash flickered. The only movement came from the steady flow of blood leaking through her fingers.

Panicked, she slapped his face. The imprint of her hand barely registered on his skin, but that wasn't the worst of it. His lips were turning blue. He wasn't breathing.

Sarah propped his head on a rock and measured the distance to the nearest bank. She had to get him to shore, and fast.

She jumped to her feet and hauled on his arms, but he was totally deadweight. Panting, she stared down the length of him, trying to think. White water churned around his body, leaching it of heat. The skin covering his chest was unbroken, but if he were bleeding inside, moving him would be the worst thing she could do. Yet if she didn't get him out of the freezing cold and breathing soon, he'd die for sure.

Sarah leapt across his body and ripped off his boots, flinging them to shore. Returning to her previous position behind his head, she crouched and wormed her hands beneath his shoulders. Rough rocks scraped her knuckles. Grimacing, she lifted up.

Lord, he was heavy.

She got her legs under her, hooked her hands under his arms and reached across his chest, linking her fingers for maximum leverage. Gritting her teeth, she hoisted him into a sitting position.

His head lolled, sending blood-tinted water cascading down the front of her petticoat. She gasped at the drenching her legs received and pulled backward, fighting for purchase on the wet rocks.

He slid a couple of inches. She looked skyward and threw all her weight back, using every muscle she possessed. Another couple of inches. At this rate, it would take forever.

"Butcher!" she cried.

The dog bounded forward.

"Pull!"

To show him what she wanted, she jammed her feet into the rocky creek bed and strained back with such ferocity, sweat sprang out on her forehead. One step, torturous and slow. Two. How much time had passed since Zach had fallen in? Fifty heartbeats? A hundred?

"Help," she shouted, scrambling for a better foothold.

Butcher grabbed a mouthful of material at Zach's hip. Following her lead, he tugged with his massive jaws. Together, they pulled. Her arms felt like they were being torn from their sockets. Stones bit between her churning feet. Afraid to stop and lose momentum, she blocked out the pain by counting her steps.

"Three...four...five...six..."

The back of her heels collided with solid mud. Staggering, she glanced sideways and saw she'd reached the overhang that marked the shore. She heaved one last time and laid Zach down on the bank. For all intents and purposes, he was half in the water and half out, but the positioning would have to do. At least most of him was on dry ground.

Blood ran freely across his forehead but she couldn't worry about that now. She crouched by his side and pressed her ear to his chest. His heartbeat was strong, thank the Lord.

Energized, she forced a hand behind his neck and quickly checked his mouth for debris, recalling the steps Papa had taught her long ago. Resuscitation, he'd called it. Something she should learn, since she loved to swim with her friends in Birch Pond.

She pinched Zach's nose with her fingers, took a steadying breath, bent over him and fit her mouth around his.

His lips were so cold. Exhaling, she lifted her head and gulped more air. A minute ago those lips had been grinning at her. Surely someone so full of life could not be so easily erased from existence.

Help me, Lord. He's too young to die.

Using what she hoped was a natural rhythm, Sarah bent over him again and again, keeping a sharp eye on the rise and fall of his chest.

Butcher hovered nearby, pacing and growling. He did not take kindly to strangers, especially when they got close to her. Between breaths, Sarah called him off and he slunk away to stand guard by the nearest tree. She fingered the pulse on Zach's neck. Was it her imagination, or had his heartbeat slowed?

Afraid she had been too timid before, she thrust his chin higher and forced in a great lungful of air. Beneath her fingers, the corded muscles of his throat tightened. Sarah pulled back, but nothing happened.

"Breathe!" She grabbed his shoulders and shook him, desperate for some sign of life. To her profound relief, he coughed.

Quickly she shoved him onto his side and pounded between his shoulder blades. He curled up in a fetal position and coughed again, hacking out mucus. Muddy water flooded from his lungs, mixing with blood from his wound, her next concern.

Sarah scanned the lush weeds that grew along the creek. Spotting what she was looking for, she got up, grabbed a handful of bright green yarrow and stuffed it into her mouth.

He groaned and rolled onto his back, choking and wheezing. She knelt beside him, pushed him onto his side so he faced away from her, and forced him to stay that way by placing her knees along his spine. Spitting the chewed yarrow into her hand, she reached over his shoulder and groped along his hairline, blindly looking for the wound.

Entangled in his belt was her discarded chemise. With her free hand, she wrung it out as best she could while she packed yarrow into the wound and covered the whole with the chemise, using it like a pressure bandage. He'd need stitching eventually, but first the bleeding had to be stopped.

His back muscles tensed and he gagged and spat out a mouthful of water tinged by blood. "Jesus," he said.

Startled by the evocation of His name, Sarah leaned forward to better see Zach's face. His previous manner did not bespeak a God-fearing man. Tension ridged his jaw. He must be in considerable pain.

"Shh," she said, decreasing the pressure on the makeshift bandage. "You'll be all right now."

Zach barely heard her. The pounding of his heart filled not only his ears but his vision, making him feel as if he were swirling madly in a red vortex. Words were nothing but bits of flotsam floating on the surface, but he grabbed for them anyway, propelled by the fear of being swept down under. He tried to speak. What came out was a guttural groan even he didn't recognize.

"You've coughed up a lot of water. Try swallowing and see if that helps your throat."

He obeyed and gagged on his own tongue. "Hurts," he managed.

"Where does it hurt?"

Mists cleared from his mind, leaving him aware of his surroundings. He was lying on hard ground, curled on his right side. Someone leaned over him from behind. He could feel the knees pressed up against his back to keep him from rolling over.

"Sarah?"

"You remember," she said. "That's a good sign."

Why her name popped into his mind, he didn't know. But her voice was calm and overrode the feeling of being in a bad dream. Grateful for the point of reference, he opened his eyes. Matted grass came into focus. Beyond that was a swirl of whitewater studded by rocks. Something heavy was coming down on top of his head. The heat created there made him realize how cold he felt everywhere else, especially from the waist down. "Numb," he said.

Sarah pressed her chest along his exposed side, draping him with what little body heat she had. His skin was damp and cool to the touch, robbing her of breath. Gooseflesh sprang up on her upper arms. Her nipples hardened. She bit her lip and hoped he wasn't conscious enough to notice.

Zach discovered that if he moved his eyes to the left, he could look far enough sideways to make out a face hovering just above him. "Cold," he said, needing her to understand. "Too cold."

She nodded. "I know. I'll get you a blanket as soon as I stop the bleeding."

He relaxed somewhat, thankful she knew something about the dangers of hypothermia. "What...happened?"

"You fell into the creek."

Her words conjured up fragmented pictures of water and rocks and an overwhelming sense of nausea. He closed his eyes and swallowed. "I need to get up."

"Not yet. You're bleeding too much."

"I need to. Right now." He tried to lever himself into a sitting position.

"No!"

She rocked forward, pinning him down with the top half of her body. Zach struggled to shrug off her weight. Slight though she was, he couldn't get her to budge. Disgusted by his weakness, he pushed at her, anyway, because he needed the distraction she provided. If he wasn't careful, he was going to be violently ill.

"Stop it! You're making the bleeding worse!"

"Damn you," he whispered, and gave up, swallowing sickly.

"Here." Keeping pressure on his head, she shifted and he heard a tearing sound of leaves being stripped from their stems. "Chew on this," she said. "It will help the feeling pass."

When he opened his mouth to ask what it was, she stuffed the leaves inside. A fresh minty taste cut through his senses. He resisted his first instinct to spit the stuff out and chewed slowly. The nausea gradually subsided. After a few minutes he spit it out and glanced sideways at her, feeling considerably better. Aside from the pounding in his head and mild shock, he seemed to be all in one piece.

"What was that?" he asked.

"Catnip."

"You had me eating *what?*"

"It's a plant from the mint family. Not only does it soothe your stomach, it has a mild sedative effect."

"Don't tell me you're one of those granola heads from Boulder."

"I beg your pardon?"

"You know. A hippie type. Homeopath. New Ager." When she still looked blank, he said, "Someone who gets cosmic meaning out of gathering herbs and making them into medicines and stuff."

"I have some knowledge of herbal remedies," she said, frowning down at him. "Do you feel better?"

He did, amazingly so, but he wasn't ready to admit it, not when she looked so worried. Things were coming back to him now. He'd been trying to make a move on this woman. Seeing her big mild eyes and the lush lower lip caught by her teeth, he could understand why. He decided to milk her sympathy for all it was worth. "I remember my horse got spooked. Is she all right?"

"She ran off before I could catch her. Butcher frightened her rather thoroughly, I'm afraid."

"Butcher?"

"My dog."

"The vicious animal that attacked me belongs to you?"

"He's not truly vicious. He was only trying to protect me."

"By going for my jugular? You have him tied up, I hope."

"I told him to stay by the tree and he will. He is highly trained."

"Trained for what? Combat?"

"He didn't cause your injury. When you fell, you hit your head on a rock."

Zach gingerly raised his hand to investigate. Her slim fingers covered a warm, wet cloth that was clamped to his forehead like a vise. "How bad is it?"

"I haven't been able to stop the bleeding. The cut is about the length of a finger."

"How long have I been out?"

"Out?" Sarah asked, confused by the context in which he used the word.

"Unconscious."

"Only a few minutes."

"Bad enough I got bucked off my horse on my first ride out on the range. But knocked out, too? The boys at the bunkhouse will never let me live this one down."

So he felt well enough to rue what had happened. Sarah craned her neck and checked his pupils, looking to see if both were the same size. They were, indicating there was no bleeding inside the head. That was the most dangerous injury of all.

Healthy color was returning to his cheeks. Awed by his recuperative powers, she peeked beneath the makeshift bandage. In spite of the yarrow poultice, blood still welled from the wound. She clamped down again, harder this time.

"Ow!"

"Sorry. The bleeding won't stop unless there is constant pressure."

"You a nurse, too?"

"Not a professional one."

"Where did you learn all this stuff?"

She shrugged, scarcely knowing what to tell him. For years she'd nursed her mother through various illnesses, but this she couldn't explain without raising further questions. Zach already knew far too much about her as it was. "Where I come from, everyone is taught the various properties of herbs."

"Where is that?"

"A very small town. I'm sure you've never heard of it."

"Try me."

"It's many miles away."

"All the more reason for you to tell me. I've traveled to some pretty far places."

"You have?" she asked, determined to turn the subject. "I thought you said you owned this ranch."

"In a manner of speaking. Someone else has always managed it. I left home a long time ago."

"You left by choice?" Sarah asked, disbelieving. Where she came from, men never gave up their birthright.

"Why does that surprise you?"

"There are few possessions more precious than land."

"You sound like my dad. When I was growing up, he mortgaged everything to keep hold of this place. You know what it got him? A belly full of ulcers and a fatal heart attack at the age of forty-nine. You think I want that for myself?"

"I'm sorry to hear of your father's death. Mine, too, died when I was young, before his time. But you were born of this land. It is in your blood."

"I'm here only because I finally convinced the rest of my family to sell. I can't wait to get rid of it."

His vehemence surprised her, especially considering his cowboy aura of being one with the land. "But you ride as well as any man I've ever seen. You obviously have a way with horses."

"There's more to ranching than horses."

"It's in the way you hold yourself, your hands, your eyes—"

"Now I know you're from Boulder," he interrupted. "Next thing you know, you'll be telling me we've met in a former life."

"I beg your pardon?"

"Never mind. I remember falling into the water but not much else. Who pulled me out?"

"I did." He felt along her wrists, measuring them between a long, callused forefinger and thumb. She swallowed, more certain than ever he worked with his hands. They were the essence of strength.

"You couldn't have pulled me out by yourself," he said. "What do you weigh—a hundred pounds soaking wet? I'm six-four and a solid two ten."

He was indeed solid. The powerful muscles against her breasts told her that. Shamed by her awareness, Sarah shifted her weight, trying to hide the fact that significant parts of her anatomy were quite naked. "Butcher helped."

"No wonder I feel chewed up. You weren't hurt yourself, were you? My horse didn't run you down?"

"No, nothing like that," she said, unwilling to mention the cuts on her feet or her bruised knuckles. They were trivial hurts compared to what he'd been through.

"Then why are you shaking?"

A fine tremor, caused by the strain of holding the bandage in place for so long, shook her arms. "I'm fine."

"Are you cold?"

"Not at all." It wasn't precisely a lie. The heat created between her body and his was keeping her very warm indeed. In spite of his injury, he radiated a disturbing vitality.

"Does the sight of blood bother you?"

"My arms are tired, is all."

"Move, then. I'll hold the bandage for a while."

"The pressure must be constant or the bleeding will worsen."

"Give yourself a break, Sarah. You can't be comfortable sitting behind me with your arms extended like that. You're shaking like a leaf."

"I'm fine."

"Come sit here," he said, patting the trampled grass in front of him. "You'll cramp up for sure if you don't change your position."

Sarah scrunched down farther to prove to him that she could rest comfortably. The palsy in her arms lessened, but now there was considerable pressure on her spine, which was forced to arch unnaturally to keep the upper half of her body hidden from his sight. "There. I feel much better."

"Yeah, right. I can feel your knees against my back. You must be all doubled over like a pretzel."

"I'm fine, truly."

"Damn it, Sarah. Get your butt in gear or I'll move you myself."

A jolt went through her as he groped backward, brushing her arm. His foul language was equally unnerving, though she ought to be inured to hearing such things. Over the course of her journey, she'd worked among people who'd used far worse four-letter words in everyday conversation.

"Did you hear me?"

Blunt fingers grazed the damp waistband of her petticoat. She bit her lip, able to do little more than squirm as he explored her clothed hip and the bared stretch of skin covering her ribs. To her utter chagrin, he chuckled. When next he spoke, she could tell by his tone that he'd realized the extent of her predicament.

"I think I understand your problem. This bandage used to be your top, right?"

Unable to see the humor in the situation, Sarah put even more pressure on her spine, hoping to block his hand from further exploration. "I told you," she retorted. "I am quite fine."

"Me, too. In fact, I'm feeling better and better." In spite of the awkward angle, he groped again, coming perilously close to her breasts.

"Stop rummaging around my... my bosom."

He burst out laughing. "Bosom? Where did you get a word like that?"

"It's a perfectly natural word," she said through gritted teeth.

"Natural, my eye. Who are you, Sarah? A nun who's lost her way to the convent?"

"Remove your hand immediately, sir, or I'll make you very sorry you survived your dunking in the creek," she grated, emphasizing each syllable.

"Not until you take my advice and move your nicely shaped rear over here." He caressed her hip in a most familiar gesture, thoroughly enjoying himself. "I'm waiting."

He'd certainly made a quick recovery, Sarah thought, grimacing. Not only was he built like the proverbial ox, he had the manners of one, too. Worse, she couldn't avoid disgracing herself unless she released her hold on the bandage. He might deserve such treatment, but if his wound continued to bleed as it had been wont to do, she'd have a bigger problem than mere embarrassment to deal with. "Very well," she said. "If you remove your hand, I will move my rear, as you so indelicately put it. But only if you close your eyes," she tacked on, wanting him to prove he was trustworthy.

"And miss the treat of a lifetime?"

"You won't do it?"

"No way."

Sarah had heard that expression before during her journey, and knew what it meant. The stubborn goat. After all
she'd done, too. "Why must you be so bullheaded?"

"Had some experience with bulls, have you, Sarah?"

"Like most males of their species, they always want to do
exactly as they please."

"Wouldn't be a bull otherwise. Be a steer headed for the
slaughterhouse. Ever think of that?"

"You're talking nonsense."

"You wouldn't call it nonsense if you were the steer."

Sarah bit her lip, struggling to hold on to her composure.
Steers, indeed. She tried a different tack. "If I may be so
bold as to remind you, I'm in this position not for my
health, but yours. All I ask is that you comply with a simple request."

"Nice try, Sarah." He chuckled, patting her hip.

"Why won't you grant me this one favor?"

"Give me one good reason why I should," he said sug-
gestively, running a wayward finger along the waistband of
her petticoat.

"Because," she blurted, "I pulled you out of the water
and got you breathing again!"

"What?" His finger stopped.

"Did you know I lost my shoes in that creek? My chemise is ruined, not to mention my petticoat."

"What did you say?"

"I said, I'll never be able to wear these undergarments
again! And my only decent pair of shoes are halfway to
kingdom come by now!"

"No, before that. Did you really give me mouth-to-
mouth?"

Sarah blinked in consternation. Mouth-to-mouth described it very well, indeed. Undoubtedly he'd tease her unmercifully about this liberty, as well. "I beg your pardon?"

"Quit begging my pardon and give me a straight answer for once," he said. "Did you or did you not give me mouth-to-mouth resuscitation?"

"You weren't breathing," she said miserably.

"Let me get this straight. My horse bucks me off and I do a face plant in the creek, knocking myself out while cutting my head open. You come over, drag me out, get me breathing again and sop up half my bodily fluids with your underwear. Does that about cover it?"

"I think so," she said, catching the gist of his slang. Or so she thought until he slanted his gaze to better look at her. There were no devils in his eyes now.

"You saved my life."

Sarah swallowed, recalling an old legend of the Northern Cheyenne that said when you saved a man from death, he was beholden to you until he returned the favor. "If I had been the one to fall into the creek, you would have done the same for me."

"That's a pretty incredible statement, lady. Precious few people nowadays would go out of their way to save anybody—friend, relative, or stranger."

Sarah remembered the elderly couple who had found her collapsed by the side of the road, exhausted after seven hours of running to put distance between herself and the Community. They'd taken her home, given her food and shelter for the two days it had taken her to recover, then given her a lift to Helena, sixty miles south. "You're wrong, Zach."

"Where the hell do you come from? La-la land?"

Hearing his contempt, she felt a shrinking around her heart. "Montana," she said quietly.

"Even Montana doesn't grow them like you. What's your game?"

"Game?"

"What do you want from me?"

"We've barely met. There is nothing I could want."

"Nothing, she says. Where have I heard that before?"

"What was I supposed to do?" she inquired tartly. "Leave you to drown?"

Swearing, he jerked his head forward and faced straight ahead, wrestling with some inner demon she couldn't see. Sarah knew every living being had a personal cross to bear. But his was all the more awful for the restraint in which he held it. She had the oddest impulse to lay her cheek against his shoulder then, in silent empathy. But she held back, made uncertain by his sudden, inexplicable rage.

"I'm sorry," she said, offering the only comfort she dared.

He stiffened. "Christ, lady. Don't do me any more favors."

"I don't understand. Have I offended you?"

"Forget it. It's nothing."

"But you're upset."

"I said to forget it!"

Sarah heard the angry warning in his tone and hesitated. She still had much to learn about the world outside the Community. The relations between men and women, so prescribed in the place where she grew up, were vastly different here.

She studied the bunched line of his jaw and the fixed eyes, staring straight ahead. Yes, Zach Masterson played the renegade. But underneath there was a man possessed by something deeper—the wildness of youth. He made her think of a lonely eagle, circling in a sky full of thunderclouds.

Three

Zach lay on the creek bank with every muscle tensed, senses honed on Sarah. The silence stretched between them like a rubber band. He kept waiting for it to snap.

Where were the arguments, the demands, the recriminations? Wasn't she going to beg and plead that he close his eyes?

Apparently not, for she laid her forehead against his shoulder. The gesture was brief, wordless, and affected him in savage ways. What in hell did she think she was doing?

"I'm going to move now," she said.

His heart picked up speed. The twin knobs of her knees retreated from his spine, taking away her warmth. The pressure on the bandage shifted and he heard the crunch of gravel as she rose. The hem of her petticoat passed like a ghost over his exposed left side. Air stirred, cooling the space in the middle of his chest where sweat had broken out.

Cold sweat.

He kept his eyes wide open, holding on to his pride. The fact that he focused on a blade of grass directly in front of him meant nothing. Absolutely nothing.

She nudged his hand aside with a tentative toe. Then came the brush of damp fabric as she settled, positioning herself next to his head. "Zach?" she asked.

"What?"

"I feel much more comfortable now. Thank you."

He didn't like what those last two words did to him. It was like salt rubbed on a wound. He should be thanking her, not the other way around. But the words stuck in his craw and his unreasonable anger doubled, spurred by this gratitude that he hadn't asked for and didn't want.

It wasn't that he resented the fact she'd saved his life. Far from it. What he resented was that he owed her. Big time. And he hated, hated with a passion, owing anybody anything.

To make matters worse, telltale heat flushed the places on his body she had touched in passing. Even now he was imagining how she must look, sitting there prim and proper...and totally topless. Under ordinary circumstances, he would have discharged his sexual tension with a joke. But he couldn't even do that. Her show of dignity deserved a token gesture in return, however grudging it might be.

Zach closed his eyes.

"Bleeding stop yet?" he asked curtly.

"I dare not take the pressure off long enough to look. You've already lost too much blood."

"But I'm okay now," he said, wanting nothing more than to get away from her so he could breathe something other than the fragrance of yucca and mint. Maybe that would clear the pounding in his skull.

"I will check." The bandage slowly peeled off.

"Well?"

"Much improved. Let me dress the wound to keep it from reopening."

The rip of fabric told him she was tearing strips from her petticoat. Just what he needed to fire his imagination. "Don't you have anything else you can use?"

"My gray dress is wool and won't tear easily. I suppose my calico blouse would suffice, but then I'll only have one blouse."

"Never mind."

"No, you're right. The calico is freshly washed. I'll get it."

She rose with a soft rustle. He reached out blind and grabbed her ankle. She had incredible bone structure, delicate yet strong, like a Thoroughbred's. "What you have now is fine."

"Zach, don't be silly. You are entirely correct. Cleanliness is very important with this type of wound."

She tried to step out of his grasp. He tightened his grip, warning her to comply. "I won't let you rip up any more of your clothes."

"It's no trouble."

"It is for me."

"If the wound should become infected, I would never forgive myself."

"Let me worry about that."

"But—"

"I mean it, Sarah. The last thing I need is another sacrifice on your part."

Her ankle flexed and he felt the sweep of her petticoat brush his arm as she knelt and laid a gentle hand against the side of his face. "Zach, please. You needn't feel obliged."

Those words instantly doubled his sense of obligation. He clenched his teeth, wanting to lash out at her. But how could he lash out at someone who had just saved his life?

She ran a finger along the tight line of his jaw and sighed. The sound was soft, like her name, and for some stupid reason made him want to give in. She beat him to it. "Very well," she said. "I'll use the strips I already took from my petticoat."

He released her immediately, afraid that if he wasn't careful she'd guess the extent of the power she had over him. It didn't help that he was attracted to her physically. The more he told himself that going after her was impossible now, that he couldn't have her, that the stakes had suddenly become way too high, the more angry he became. "Hurry up," he said irritably.

She applied the strips and wound them around his head, humming under her breath. The tune was "Amazing Grace," one of the few hymns he knew because he had the Judy Collins version on tape. When he got back to Brazil, he was going to throw it away.

When she finished, he sat up abruptly, keeping his eyes closed, and waved off her attempts to help. "I'm fine," he said, despite the vertigo washing over him. "Get some clothes on."

She padded away, only to return a moment later. A warm tin cup was pressed into his hands. "Willow-bark tea," she said.

"Go get some clothes on!"

This time she hustled away, leaving the scent of woodsmoke in her wake. Scowling, he sipped the tea, knowing full well he needed both warmth and liquids. A blanket settled around his shoulders.

"Sarah!"

"I told you," she said, her voice lilting. "Bullheaded."

Zach wanted to go after her, pull her down and let her know just how bullheaded he could be. Instead he hunched under the blanket. The sooner he got warm, the sooner he'd be able to get back on his feet and get away from her.

Damn, he was dizzy. His constant shivering didn't help, but it was a good sign, indicating that his core body temperature was still within the range of normal. The loss of blood he could deal with, as long as he didn't go into major shock. Moving around would help.

"You decent yet?" he called.

"Yes," she said, sounding very close.

Startled, Zach opened his eyes. She was kneeling right in front of him, wearing the gray dress. It had a high collar and long sleeves and covered her body completely, from neck to toe. The row of shiny jet buttons down the front followed her curves, making him think of what lay beneath. "That's quite a dress," he said, and tossed back the rest of his tea.

"It's a bit formal, I know."

"Yeah? Well, you look like you're ready for my funeral."

"Not if I can help it." She held out his shirt. "I found this next to the creek. It's still fairly dry."

He grunted an unintelligible thank-you, dropped the blanket then took the shirt and gingerly pulled it over his head. She stretched the ribbed neckline so it wouldn't come in contact with his wound and her fingers grazed his ear. Zach pretended not to notice.

She fussed with the material, pulling it down over his chin. He caught her hand, forcing her to stop. "Why don't you wear jeans like everybody else?" he asked.

"You're not wearing them."

"At least my fatigues cover my legs."

"Skirts are cooler in summer, warmer in winter."

"They're also impractical as hell. Don't you have something more sensible than a heavy wool dress that looks like something my grandmother wore?"

"My other clothes are still damp."

"So is this," he observed, catching the cuff of her sleeve. He rubbed it between his fingers, measuring the level of saturation. "Not exactly drip-dry."

She shrugged. "I'll be warm enough. Wool keeps moisture away from the skin better than cotton."

It was true, but he was surprised she knew it. More brownie points. Why couldn't she have been an incompetent greenhorn? Then he could dismiss the fact that she'd saved his life as a stroke of pure luck, a quirk of fate. Quirks of fate didn't require much in the way of payback.

He pulled at his shirt and discovered one sleeve was inside out. He fiddled with it but couldn't get it right and cursed because Sarah was right next to him and he felt like a fool. Wordlessly, she guided his hand through the armhole, then ducked to pull the shirt's hem down. Her fingers brushed the skin at his waist and he experienced an insane urge to trap her hands there, to keep her close. He suddenly was glad he'd lost so much blood. It had the same effect on his sex as an icy shower.

"There," she said, stepping back. "You're all dressed."

"Whoopee."

"Here," she offered, taking his arm. "I'll help you to stand."

He shook her off and rose, gaining his balance through sheer will. Still she hovered, making him feel like an invalid. Which, judging by the unsteadiness of his legs, he was.

"Are you certain you're all right?"

"Peachy," he said, though he was about to keel over with dizziness. He focused on the nearest tree and headed toward it, concentrating on putting one foot in front of the other. Sarah stayed with him like a shadow. He wanted to tell her to go away, but if he fainted while he said it, he'd never get rid of her.

The dog trotted over to investigate. Zach put a hand on the tree to steady himself. Butcher was aptly named. He had a scarred black face and the type of long brown legs that ate up distance with ease. The eyes were small and he carried his head low, like a scouting wolf. His ears were cropped, however, and so was the tail, giving him the look of a bear somehow. Maybe it was the muscular body.

"Don't you like dogs?" she asked.

"I like them fine. Tie him up, will you?"

"Butcher just wants to make friends."

"He had his chance."

"But he won't hurt you."

Zach caught Sarah's arm. "Tie him up."

She gazed at him a long moment, her eyes a shade darker than the bark of the tree. "If you insist."

He released her, feeling dizzier than ever. Using a rope she pulled out of her pack, she attached one end to the dog's collar while wrapping the other around the base of a tree on the opposite side of the campsite. Zach studied Butcher's build to distract himself from Sarah's efficient competence. She could tie a knot better than a marine. "Pit bull cross with a beagle?" he asked.

"Pit bull father, hound mother. He can pick up a deer scent from a mile away."

"He didn't pick up on me that quick."

She scratched behind Butcher's ears, her smile serene and damned irritating. "He was hunting."

"Hunting what?"

"Supper." She walked to a heap of brown fur that lay crumpled at the edge of the clearing and picked it up. It was a dead rabbit. "That's why you didn't hear him coming when you were on your horse. He didn't bark because he had this in his mouth."

She wrapped a cord around the rabbit's hind feet and strung it from a branch. Using tongs, she selected one of the simmering tin cans set on the grate. "More tea?"

Now that her hands weren't busy, he noticed her knuckles were rubbed raw. "You told me you weren't hurt."

"My injuries are minor compared to yours. I'll tend to them later."

"You've got something else besides skinned knuckles?"

She poured tea into her own cup and sipped, her expressive eyes hesitant as she considered him over the rim. Zach frowned. She wouldn't be so reluctant unless she had more than an insignificant scratch.

"Show me, Sarah."

She held out her cup and he took it without speaking. Her hands went to the front of her skirt, hitching it up. She lifted one fine-boned foot, then the other. The abrasions weren't deep, but there were a lot of them, all over the soles of her feet, and he remembered what she'd said about losing her shoes in the creek.

"Don't you have anything you can wear besides those old Nike sneakers?"

She dropped her skirt. "They were my only pair of shoes."

"Are you kidding me?" Zach wanted to throttle her. However much she knew about living off the land, she had no business being out here by herself with little more than a pair of battered sneakers and a couple of long gowns. "How old are you?"

"Four and twenty."

"I'm surprised you've managed to live that long," he said, struck again by her way of putting things. He was also struck by a wave of pure protectiveness. If the woman didn't have sense enough to take care of herself, he'd do it himself. "Where are my boots?"

"I set them by the fire to dry."

"You'll be wearing them when we walk out of here."

She looked startled.

"They're way too big, I know, but it's only a couple of miles back to the main part of the ranch. Once we get there, I'll replace everything you've lost. The sneakers, the clothes, everything."

"You don't have to do that."

"Yes, I do."

"Zach, you don't understand. I can't go with you. I must keep moving."

"Because of this man you're so spooked about? Who the hell is he?"

"My stepfather."

She said it so matter-of-factly, Zach was sure she was pulling his leg. "Certainly a stepfather would not pose a threat to someone as old as you are."

"Maybe not in most places. But he considers me his property, to do with as he pleases."

Zach rolled his eyes. "I'm tired of arguing. You're coming with me."

"But—"

He tipped her chin up, forcing her to look at him so she would see how serious he was. "I refuse to let you hurt your feet any more than you already have."

She nodded and ran the tip of her tongue around her mouth. It was a nervous gesture, and one that drew his attention. Actually, he liked her better this way. A little off balance, a little unsure. "That's most kind of you," she said.

His motivation had hardly been kindness, but he let it pass. The look of her mouth made that imperative. He dropped his hand and leaned against the tree, feigning indifference. "I owe you a lot. Five hundred dollars should do it for the clothes. As for my life, well, I guess you can't blame me for wanting to put a somewhat higher price tag on that. Does ten thousand sound fair to you?"

"Ten thousand dollars?"

The raw shock on her face told him she hadn't expected such a windfall. "Don't look so surprised," he said. "I'm good for it."

"It's not that I doubt you possess such a sum. Anyone who owns a ranch is a rich man, indeed."

"The money has nothing to do with the ranch. Ever since I left home, I've been traveling around the world, working as I go and socking away the dough, just to prove to my old man that I wasn't the bum he said I was. After thirteen-some years, it's added up."

"I'm sure it has. Nevertheless, it is not something I require."

"Think of it as a token of my appreciation."

"Ten thousand dollars is more than a mere token, Zach."

"For you, maybe. Not for me."

The barb put a little extra starch in her spine. "Nevertheless," she said stiffly, "I cannot take your money."

"Sure you can. You already said you would."

"I said you may replace the things I lost. My shoes and chemise are worth perhaps fifty dollars, if that."

"Use the ten grand to buy twenty pairs of shoes and a hundred of those chemise things, I don't care. It's yours."

"Must I be ungracious in order for you to understand? *I don't need it.*"

"Give it to your favorite charity if you want."

"Is that why you think it necessary to offer such a sum? That because my clothes are ragged, I'm a charity case?"

"If the shoe fits..." He shrugged. "We'll settle up as soon as we get to the ranch."

Her cheeks reddened but Zach refused to let guilt get to him. She was too damned righteous for her own good.

"Why are you doing this?" she demanded.

"Because I can."

He saw the righteousness shift in her eyes, becoming something dark and utterly cool. "You mean to drag me back to your ranch against my will?"

Her voice was full of steel. It made him feel put down, reprimanded, as though he were schoolboy to her teacher. He wanted it the other way around. In fact, he wanted her to be scared. That way, she'd maintain the distance between them. She was a woman alone, and if she didn't recognize the danger she was in, he'd give her a taste of it. If he were lucky, he'd at last find something about her he didn't like and kill two birds with one stone. "Sarah," he drawled, "it won't be against your will."

"I have told you quite clearly that I have no intention of going with you. Now, will you excuse me? I'd best be on my way."

"I don't think so." He caught her arm.

"Unhand me, sir."

"Not until I get what I want."

"And what is it you want?"

His smile was infuriating. "You."

"All right," Sarah snapped, figuring a lie to be the lesser of two evils. "I'll accompany you back to the ranch. We will discuss the issue of reward there. Now, will you let me go?"

"Sarah, I'm surprised at you. A promise made under duress is no promise at all."

"I give you my word," she said through her teeth.

"I need something better than that. Seal your promise with a kiss."

"I'd rather kiss a snake." She pulled away.

His grip tightened. "That can be arranged."

She thought at first he was joking, but when she checked his face, she suddenly wasn't sure. His expression had hardened into vengeful lines. "Why are you treating me with such contempt?"

The truth stung, but Zach had the advantage physically, and he felt driven to prove it, both to her and to himself. In one lightning movement he pinned her against the tree. She gasped at the rough contact and he leaned into the sound, seeking it. She squirmed, but he'd planned the attack well and a rush of adrenaline gave him more strength than an injured man had right to expect. Credit Sarah's fortuitous zeal, he thought as his mouth came down on hers, and her damned yucca perfume.

Butcher barked wildly. Zach ignored the dog, using lips and teeth to expand the kiss into a thorough sampling of the tender skin of her neck.

"Stop it!" she cried.

He nuzzled his way to her ear, tonguing it. Shuddering, she fought in earnest, punching and twisting in a way that served to make him more determined. There was a certain satisfaction in knowing he could taste Sarah like this, at will, especially since she was so damned good at making him feel like she was more in control of the situation than he was.

"Yo!"

At the sound of the shout, Sarah broke away and ran to Butcher, untying him from the tree. Keeping hold of his collar, she quieted him and craned her neck to look beyond the trees.

"Who is it?" Zach asked.

She spared him a withering glance. "Two men on horseback, riding this way. They're leading a third horse." She paused a long moment and shaded her eyes, straining to see in the growing dusk. "I believe it's yours, though they're too far away to tell for sure."

"Must be the cavalry," he said, realizing Coburn would have put out a search when the buckskin returned without a rider. "Get your things together, Sarah."

"I would never go with you now."

"Don't be stupid. You can't stay here all by yourself."

"I won't be staying here. I told you I'd be off your land by nightfall."

"The sun is about to set. You're going to walk in the dark, without shoes on?"

"I've done it before."

Somehow he didn't doubt she had. "I'm not giving you a choice," he noted pointedly, unsure why he needed to rub it in. If Sarah had been a man, he wouldn't have. "Let me repeat. Those men on horseback are my ranch hands. There's three of us and only one of you."

"There is Butcher."

"Which would you bet on? A dog and a woman on foot or three men on horseback?"

She answered by stripping her pack from the tree branch and bending to gather her gear with a quiet determination he didn't quite trust, like a heifer looking to bolt.

"Don't even think about it," Zach warned.

"Think about what?"

"Leaving without me."

She stopped packing to look at him. "So you fancy yourself a mind reader, as well, Mr. Masterson?"

"No, not a mind reader. A student of human nature."

A hearty male voice called out. "Zach!"

"Hey, Coburn. Miller," Zach said without taking his eyes off Sarah. Her gaze never wavered. Damn, she was stubborn. Despite his annoyance, he allowed her a small victory by looking away first.

"So this is where you've been hiding." Coburn trotted up the embankment on a flashy Appaloosa, his face creased with worry. Behind him rode Miller on a brown-and-white pinto, leading Nutkin.

"Took a spill," said Zach.

"You hurt bad?"

"Just a little bump to the head."

"Me and the boys figured something went wrong. The buckskin came back all lathered up."

"She okay?"

"Brought her along, didn't I? Think you can ride back?"

"Long as we go slow." Zach caught the mare's bridle and ran his hand down her neck. She didn't quiver this time. All the fight had been spooked out of her.

"What the hell happened?" Miller asked.

"She threw a hissy fit in the middle of the creek and bucked me off."

"Looks like she plowed right through you, too," observed Coburn, dismounting to have a look at Zach's head.

"I hit a rock. Knocked me out for a time. Sarah pulled me out of the water and patched me up."

"That itty-bitty thing we saw when we first rode up?"

"Yeah. She's camped here."

"Not anymore," said Miller.

Zach checked the campsite and swore. Sarah had disappeared. The fire was out, and the grate, tarp and blanket were gone. He scanned the ridge. Halfway up the steep hill she strode, gray skirt flapping in the wind, the leather pack strapped to her back. Butcher bounded ahead of her, leading the way.

"You want me to go after her, boss?"

Enraged that she'd gotten by him without so much as a sound, Zach pulled on his boots and mounted the buckskin. He reined in, suppressing his first impulse to spur his horse in hot pursuit. First of all, he'd probably fall flat on his face. Second, he should be glad she'd left. Real glad. Her abrupt departure meant he didn't owe her a thing. "No," he said. "If she wants to go that bad, let her."

"What was she doing here?"

"Damned if I know."

"Look here, boss. What about this? You want to keep it?"

Miller scooped up a red rag from the ground and passed it to Zach. Thinking he would be smart to have something with him in case the wound opened up again, he folded it in two. It wasn't until he saw the lace edging the hem that he realized what the rag had once been. Her chemise.

Zach spread it out on his damp thigh, sickened by how soaked it was with blood. Only a fragment of white satin ribbon along the rounded neckline had escaped unscathed.

That one little clean spot seared him.

She had literally sacrificed the clothes on her back. In return, what had he given her? Nothing but grief. In fact, she'd been right to refuse the money. Deep down, he'd sensed the payment offer would insult her. He'd wanted to drive her away.

Zach's hand closed over the cloth, forcing it into a tight ball inside his fist. He studied the empty ridge. He'd succeeded, too. She had disappeared without a trace, leaving nothing but windswept grass and empty sky, as though she'd never existed. Except for the evidence he held, he could almost pretend that she hadn't dragged him from the creek, got him breathing again and stopped him from bleeding to death.

Almost.

Mouth grim, he tucked the ruined chemise into his back pocket and gathered the reins. "I've changed my mind. Go after her, Coburn. Put her up in the trailer until I get back from the hospital. I need to go for stitches."

"Right, boss."

"And, Coburn?"

"Yeah?"

"Beware of the dog."

Four

Sarah woke with a start. Her bed was soft, softer than she had reason to expect. She was also warm, warmer than she'd been in weeks of sleeping outdoors. One ragged wool blanket was usually not enough to ward off the chilly autumn nights. Trained after months of living by her wits, she used only her eyes and looked around the small room. Dawn was just creeping through a tiny window along the wall next to the bed.

A real window, a real wall, a real bed.

She lifted her head, felt a soreness in the muscles of her back and arms, and remembered where she was. Zach Masterson's trailer. At least, the Bar M hands had called it that. Last night, however, when she'd turned down the bedcovers, the sheets had not smelled of him.

She wouldn't have slept between them if they had.

She stretched, working the kinks from her limbs. Butcher stirred from his blanket on the floor and sniffed at the thick quilt covering her body. She gave him her hand and he wagged his tail.

"Saving a man's life sure makes for a sound sleep, doesn't it, boy?" she said, scratching behind his ears.

He blew through his nose contentedly and relaxed his muzzle on the mattress. The luxury of a pillow under her head made her relax, too. Most times she used her pack to rest on, rolled up to provide some semblance of support. The pillow was nicer. Much nicer. So were the two men who had brought her here, compared to their boss.

She frowned in the semidark, remembering. A dangerous man, Zach Masterson. A real charmer. She'd even come to trust him, after a fashion. That was the unbelievable part. She usually was a pretty good judge of character.

He'd turned on her so suddenly. The kiss had stunned her, especially when she'd come to the point of actually admiring the man. Stalwart in the face of his injury, he possessed a ready wit whatever the circumstances. And she couldn't fault him for his behavior when he'd first come upon her. She *had* been trespassing on his land.

She sat up quickly, intent on being far away from his ranch before he returned. She'd spent the night out of a sense of obligation to Mr. Coburn and Mr. Miller, who had treated her with the utmost kindness and respect. Having been persuaded that Zach would not be released from the hospital until the following day, she'd agreed to accept their offer of hospitality. They hadn't manhandled her or made her feel like a stupid child who didn't have the means or know-how to take care of herself. Unlike some people of their shared acquaintance.

Shaking her head, she checked her feet. Thanks to the buildup of calluses she'd developed over the course of so much walking during her journey, the scraped soles were not as bad as she anticipated. Retrieving her pack, she pulled out some absorbent strips of tanned rabbit skin she kept for emergencies and wrapped them around her feet, creating a pair of makeshift moccasins. Then she found her calico blouse and brown homespun skirt and dressed, wishing she had time to take another bath. The trailer's bathroom was tiny but had running water, a luxury she took advantage of whenever the opportunity presented itself. Last night she'd even washed her hair again, enjoying the rich lather of bottled shampoo.

She did scrub her face, reveling in the milled bar of store-bought soap and instant hot water. Outsiders didn't seem to appreciate these creature comforts, but having lived without them for most of her life, she did.

Next she pinned up her hair and packed her things, moving swiftly because the sky had lightened considerably. She estimated the time as being close to seven, which was well beyond the hour she usually rose. Credit a decent bed, she thought wistfully. Only God knew when she'd have the opportunity to sleep in another one.

Shouldering her pack, she spared a last look at the neatened trailer, squared her shoulders and opened the door. A blast of cold air took her breath. Frost covered the packed dirt of the yard. Until the sun got higher in the sky, she was going to have to move fast to keep warm. At least the cold ground would numb the nagging soreness of her feet.

Light spilled from the large barn next to the bunkhouse. Likely, the ranch hands were up and about, caring for the stock. Quietly ordering Butcher to heel, she limped away from the barn toward a house set off behind a row of golden-leafed cottonwoods. The windows were boarded up, affording some assurance of privacy. If she could make her way unobtrusively around to the back, she would make it off the property without incident.

She glanced around as she walked, checking to see if anyone spotted her. Her bare feet left footprints, dark against the white-dusted ground. They were not something she could hide, so she didn't try. The rising sun would take care of her tracks soon enough. Butcher wandered amid piles of rusting junk, nose to the ground, cautious about where he did his business.

Sarah smelled coffee brewing and winced. The prospect of walking miles in the cold on an empty stomach was poor comfort, indeed, especially when she remembered the dinner Mr. Coburn had fed her last night. She hadn't had such a filling meal in many a moon. To distract herself, she sped up and broke out into the sanctuary of the tall trees, well out of sight of possible prying eyes. There she let Butcher sniff among the fallen leaves while she jogged in place and studied the house.

Two stories high, with four dormer windows and a large brick chimney, it was wrapped by a wide porch, sagging in places. Torn shingles flapped precariously from the steeply pitched roof. The paint was peeling, showing streaks of weathered gray clapboards and the occasional rot of warped wood. A screen door had once covered the front entrance. Now it teetered on one hinge, threatening to fall. All the shutters were gone, giving the place an air of blank-eyed abandonment.

Despite the poor upkeep, she could see the lines were straight and true and of superior construction. How could such a grand place like this be allowed to go to such ruin? Mr. Coburn had apologized for the cramped bunkhouse where they'd eaten last night. Why didn't they live and work out of this house?

An intact picket fence closed in a wide, spacious yard perfect for child's play. There was even an old wooden swing hanging from the thick branches of a huge golden oak. On the other side, a sprawling apple tree, shorn of leaves, provided variations of shade that fell across the flagstone walk like bones from a spindly hand.

Mesmerized, she pushed through the front gate, barely heeding the rusty grind of neglected hinges. In her mind's eye, she saw the clapboards painted white and the shutters in black, while the emerald green of morning-glory vines climbed the porch rails. She walked around to the back, struck by how easily she could imagine lace at the windows and marigolds planted in boxes beneath.

Restored in her mind, the house was like one she'd seen in a picture book, evoking the smell of baking bread and harvested hay and the calm presence of a gray-haired woman on the porch steps, shucking peas with blue-veined fingers. If she listened very hard, Sarah could even hear the laughter of children.

She was reminded of the days before Cal had come, when her mother's health was good and her father was still alive. And Granny, who rounded out their little family, living with them in her declining years. Their cabin was much smaller than this, of course, one level with just six rooms. Yet the mountains had been a backdrop much as they were here, and contentment had lived in the home of her childhood, providing a feeling of camaraderie and purpose. It was a feeling Sarah deeply missed.

In the backyard she came upon a large garden, overgrown with weeds, but more recently tended than anything she had seen so far. Someone had planted flowers and vegetables the summer before last, for while the annuals were dead, the perennials still grew in wild profusion. She stopped to pick a double handful of raspberries and ate them standing on the back-porch steps, where sunbeams poured down like honey. Warming herself, she watched Butcher streak among the few remaining dried cornstalks and pumpkin vines, hunting his favorite quarry, squirrels.

The smell of earth and plants was familiar, and the chatter of early birds feeding on the straggling sunflowers made her smile. Imagine having a house and garden like this to fix up and make her own, to do with as she pleased.

Contemplative, she wrapped her arms around her waist. She couldn't envision a more satisfactory way to spend her time than to create a home in such a place. However, much as she might like to, she didn't have time to spend daydreaming. The frost melting on the ground was an inexorable reminder of the perils of her situation. The seasons were changing. She had to find a safe place to winter in. She needed a job and a place to stay, a way to support herself, a way to prepare for the future.

She also wanted to put distance between herself and a more immediate threat. Zach. In his own way, he was just as dangerous to her well-being as Cal, or the turning of the weather. He wouldn't be pleased to find her gone when he returned to the ranch. The sooner she got to the town of Boulder, the better. She might even do well to head for Denver. Though she didn't like the hustle and bustle of the big city, it was easier to hide in the hordes of people who lived there.

With a sigh, she hefted her pack and whistled for Butcher. He came running and bounded past her, eager to be off. Striding past the garden, she turned for one last look at the house. The upper story windows appeared like eyes to her, eyes in a lonely face. She couldn't help but be reminded of Zach's expression when he'd first realized the lengths she had gone to to save his life.

There had been a desolation in him, a desolation similar to what she saw here in the boarded-up windows and neglected paint. She understood loneliness. Indeed, she had lived with it every day since her father had died and her mother had withdrawn into a shell of chronic illness. The house symbolized the feeling perfectly, like a mirror held up to the face of a lost soul.

A soul Zach was about to sell.

In that light, she could understand his restiveness, his anger. She knew how difficult it was to run from your past—this she understood down to the marrow of her bones. Perhaps she should stay long enough to tell him. But they were relative strangers and he'd undoubtedly lash out at her again, and though she knew she had been able to save his life, she didn't have the strength to save his soul. Lord knew, she had enough problems keeping her own self—body and soul—together.

Resolutely she turned and entered a small orchard located behind the garden. Butcher streaked by. Ahead she could see a barbed-wire fence, and beyond that, the road. She walked steadily and heard a sigh deeper than her own whispering through the trees. She looked over her shoulder, a lump in her throat. The house was calling to her, as surely as though it possessed a voice.

"Goodbye," she whispered.

Butcher woofed, coming back to circle around her. She slogged through fallen leaves, hunched against the cold. Again she heard the sigh, like her name, singing through the trees. She tucked her chin to her chest, wiped her eyes and kept on, forcing her legs to move. It was foolish to long for something she could not have. The Elders preached that one must be careful of such yearnings, for they often led to sin. The tenth commandment made the dictate clear. *Thou shalt not covet thy neighbor's house.* She had to go now, find a town, a job, a place to live.

A place to live.

Thy neighbor's house.

Sarah stopped in her tracks. Could it be wrong to covet thy neighbor's house if he didn't live there? Indeed, if he didn't want it at all?

She turned slowly and drank in the tableau of ranch buildings, their shabbiness softened by distance. Did she dare try? She didn't have a good concept of the value of money, but certainly ten thousand dollars would go a long way toward the price of an abandoned house. Even someone as bullheaded as Zach Masterson couldn't argue with that.

But what if Cal tracked her here? She wouldn't be able to bear it if her situation put others in danger. Yet she had no way of knowing when, or even if, he would appear. Perhaps he'd given up on her. Right now, staring at the opportunity laid out in front of her, she was willing to believe anything was possible.

Sarah called Butcher, picked up her skirts and began to run, retracing her path. Armed with hope for the future, she could take on anything—Zach included. If he wanted to strike a bargain with her, she'd let him. But it wasn't going to be his money she settled for.

Sarah stood in the bunkhouse kitchen and kneaded the lump of smooth white dough set on the counter, working it with capable hands. The butter she'd added smelled rich, reminiscent of the cream with which it was made. On impulse, she pinched a bit of salt from the canister at her elbow and dropped it on her tongue just to taste the extravagance of such waste. She'd craved salt more than once in the past few months.

Pleasure filled her mouth. Flour rose in a little cloud, but she didn't mind the dusting her skirt took, even though it was newly washed. She was having too good a time. Bread-making was one of her favorite pastimes.

It had been weeks since she'd prepared a real breakfast. Fondly she eyed the implements she'd used: ceramic bowls, slotted spoons, and a wooden rolling pin identical to the one she'd used back home. What a comfort to know that some things never changed. Even the steamy air smelled the same, redolent with the fragrance of bacon and eggs, coffee and biscuits. Butcher was curled up in the corner with a belly full of table scraps, head between his front paws. Behind her came the clatter of cutlery and the busy hum of men given over to the important task of filling their stomachs.

Sarah listened and smiled. Hungry men were hungry men the world over, whether here on a modern ranch or within the rustic confines of the Community. One thing she knew how to do well was feed them.

"More coffee, gentlemen?" she asked.

Ty Coburn squinted up from his place at the head of the table, riding herd on a plate piled high. "You're spoiling us, Sarah."

"Just paying you back for a night spent under a real roof," she admitted. Out of habit, she wrapped a towel around her hand before lifting the coffeepot from a wondrous machine that took all the work out of brewing a good, clean cup of every cowhand's favorite drink. "It's been a long time since I've had the pleasure of cooking for an appreciative audience. I'd forgotten how much I enjoyed it."

"Good thing, too," piped in Mel Lawson, one of the other ranch hands. "Haven't had a breakfast like this since Mrs. Barton retired."

"Yeah, Coburn," said Jason Miller. "Those rocks you call biscuits just won't cut it anymore. Why don't we hire this here pretty lady? With all the work Masterson plans to have us do, it would be nice to have a decent meal to look forward to."

"Yeah, I'm tired of trading kitchen duty," said Mel.

Ty leaned back in his chair, his expression thoughtful. "What do you say, miss? Interested?"

"I might be," she said, careful about showing too much excitement at the unexpected boon. She'd have to retain all her wits if she was going to achieve what she wanted. "I am looking for a job."

"The hitch is, the ranch is about to be put up for sale."

"Really?" she asked, her heart picking up speed. "Zach mentioned that he'd come back here to get rid of it, but I wasn't quite sure what he meant."

"It means all the ranch hands are going to be mighty busy these next few weeks rounding up cattle and riding fences. It sure would be a lot easier if we had a hot meal to send us off in the morning and another one to look forward to at night when we came home."

"I did some cooking for line camps this summer, so I know I can handle the work. But I also need a place to stay."

"Room and board, eh?" asked Ty. "What about the trailer?"

"I thought Zach was staying there."

"If you could call it that. He likes to sleep outside unless the weather is real bad. Under the circumstances, I don't think he'll mind bunking with the men. Not once he tastes your cooking."

"What about the main house?" she countered. "I noticed it's all boarded up."

There was a small silence while the hands exchanged glances. Ty cleared his throat. "Not possible. Sorry."

"Why not?"

"No one's set foot in the place for years, Sarah. It's a real mess."

"I clean as well as I cook."

Ty shook his head. "You'll have to take it up with Zach. He's the one who boarded up the house after his father died."

"Why? It's such a grand old place."

"Ain't my right to say. What I can do, though, is offer you the hospitality of the trailer. I know it's old, but Mrs. Barton kept it pretty nice. She lived there for nigh on ten years before she retired. And if you don't mind the uncertainty of working on a place that's on the sales block, I'll talk to Zach about hiring you on. Sure would be nice to have a woman's touch around the place again."

"I'd be obliged."

The slam of a car door outside brought Butcher's head up. He woofed and sniffed the air. Sarah went to the window. A yellow car with a small sign on the roof that said Taxi was backing out of the drive. In the dust left in its wake stood Zach.

His denim jeans were so deeply black she knew they must be new. Above a plain belt buckle, a leather jacket hid much of his muscular leanness, exposing only the bronzed column of his neck. As before, he was hatless. A breeze ruffled his dark hair and he raked his hand through it. The gesture was quick, impatient.

"Speak of the devil," Ty said from his seat at the table.

Butcher barked in earnest.

"Quiet," Sarah said to the dog, and pointed to the corner where she'd laid out her wool blanket. Butcher obeyed the command but remained alert, focused on the door.

She shoved the coffeepot into its proper place with a trembling hand, aware of the import of the moment. All her plans would be for naught unless she could get Zach to agree.

The door opened. She turned around to face him squarely. The hard edges of the kitchen counter bit into the small of her back.

He'd shaved. Unaccountably, she recalled the harsh rub of whisker stubble and her cheeks burned. His gaze swept the room, landing on her. She forced herself to meet his eyes, steeling against more memories. But what hit her was the impact of the present, the restless vitality that defined Zach Masterson. The whiteness of the bandage taped across his forehead made the impact all the greater.

"You're here," he said. "Good."

"And a hearty good morning to you, too," she said, knowing she could give him no quarter. Not if she wanted to have her way. She folded her arms.

Coburn cleared his throat. "Thought we wouldn't be seeing you until this afternoon."

"You know how I can't stand hospitals. Made the doctors release me early."

"Head all right?"

"I'll live." Zach jerked his head toward the door. "I don't see a whole lot of work being done around here."

Ty's chair scraped back, squeaking on the linoleum. "We were just leaving, boss. Excuse us, Sarah."

The hands stacked their dishes in the sink, grabbed their hats and filed out in silence, one by one, each passing Zach, who barely moved aside. Coburn was last. Sarah couldn't see the older man's expression because his back was to her, but she did see him pause. A muscle on Zach's jaw tightened while he listened. Speculative blue eyes flicked in her direction.

She immediately busied herself at the sink, heat climbing higher on her cheeks. When the door finally slammed, she continued scraping dishes, waiting for him to make the first move. He stayed by the door, watching her.

"You're still mad," he said finally.

"Shouldn't I be?"

"I guess I was hoping a good night's sleep might soften you up a bit."

"You're the one who needs softening, not I."

"Ouch," he said. "She scores."

His tone teased, but underneath she sensed the first tiny indication of concession on his part. She stopped scraping plates and turned off the tap. "Would you care for a cup of coffee?" she asked, unbending a little.

"Thanks."

She retrieved a mug from a cabinet and poured the coffee, remembering this time she didn't need the towel to protect her hand.

"Does this mean I'm forgiven?" he asked when she handed him the mug.

"No."

"Sarah—" He caught her arm. Butcher reacted instantly. He lunged from the corner, snarling.

Sarah raised her hand and forestalled the dog with a sharp word. Butcher skidded to a stop but he never took his eyes off Zach.

"He gives new meaning to the phrase guard dog."

"I told you yesterday how devoted he is. I would advise you not to provoke him again."

Zach stepped back and whistled, impressed both by Butcher's protective streak and Sarah's ability to control it.

"Would a few strips of jerky be too much for him to handle?" He pulled out a package of bacon-flavored dog treats from the cabinet.

"He won't take food from your hand."

"After what I did to you yesterday, I suppose I can't blame him. Here," he said, shoving the package across the counter at her. "You give it to him."

"Neither will he take it from me. He was trained early on by someone else not to eat anything unless it's in his bowl."

"Try," he said, folding his arms, obviously skeptical.

She selected one of the strip-like dog treats and held it out. "Here, Butcher."

Zach noted how the dog's gaze shifted between him and the treat. The black muzzle lifted, showing off a nice set of fangs. "I wouldn't get too close if I were you," he commented.

"Like most of God's creatures, he would never deliberately hurt someone he loves." She sidled closer to the dog, unfazed by the growl coming low from his throat. "Don't you move, though," she said. "I can't make any guarantees about your safety, at least for the moment."

"I wouldn't dream of it," Zach said, and leaned a casual hip against the kitchen counter. However, there was nothing casual about the way he watched the interplay between the woman and the dog.

"Here, Butcher." Sarah held out the treat, coaxing him with soft words. In spite of his threatening posture, he stretched his nose toward the treat and wagged his stub of a tail. But, true to her word, he didn't take it.

"Throw it on the floor."

"Here you go, boy," she said, tossing the treat at his feet. "Show the doubting Thomas what a strong character you've got."

Butcher didn't even bother to sniff it. Instead he had eyes only for Sarah, who rewarded him with a gentle smile. He wiggled all over and came forward to be petted.

"I'll be damned," Zach said.

"I once tried to give him a slab of raw beefsteak," she said, stroking Butcher thoroughly before picking the treat up from the floor. "He wouldn't touch it."

"He must have been trained by a real expert."

"Yes," she said quietly, and washed her hands. "A real expert."

Zach raised an eyebrow. "It was him, wasn't it? Your stepfather."

"Yes."

"Is that why he's after you? You stole his dog?"

"Cal doesn't like to lose anything which belongs to him." Needing to turn the subject, she sent Butcher back to the corner and pointed toward Zach's bandage. "Your wound, has it been stitched?"

He tilted his head, lowering it fractionally. "See for yourself."

She didn't quite trust the amused expression in his eyes. He was up to something. "I don't wish to disturb the wound."

"The dressing needs to be checked every couple of hours. Won't you do the honors?"

Such a direct request was difficult to deny. Again came that niggling suspicion. But she needed to be satisfied he was quite all right, that his wound was on its way to healing. Then, Sarah told herself, she could ask to work here with a clear conscience.

She stepped forward, positioning herself in front of him. Even though he lowered his head, she had to raise herself on tiptoe to see properly and laid her hand on his shoulder to steady herself. An instant awareness shot through her palm.

Persevering, she was proud of the way she casually brushed his forelock aside and peeked beneath the loosely taped gauze. Tiny black threads bisected the nasty three-inch wound in neat intervals. A purplish bruise, hardly noticeable because of his deep tan, underscored the finely stitched line.

"The people who treated me at the hospital were amazed there were no signs of infection. That green stuff you put on worked like a charm."

"Yarrow has antiseptic as well as blood-clotting qualities."

"You'll have to show me what it looks like in plant form. Might come in handy someday."

"Do the stitches hurt?" she asked on impulse, responding to the empathetic fluttering of her stomach.

"Not anymore."

Alerted by his tone, she checked his expression and, sure enough, he was grinning like a cat who'd gotten into the cream. "I see you have recovered your sense of humor," she said primly, pressing the tape holding the bandage back into place.

"I did lose it there for a while, didn't I?"

Surprised he would admit it, she nodded and stepped away. Her awareness of him, however, stayed with her. She washed her hands again, but the cold water didn't help. "What do you do, Zach, when you're not busy selling the family ranch?"

"Wow, a personal question. I must be making progress. I'm a jack of all trades, master of none. Right now, me and my partner have a guide business taking people through the Amazon jungle."

"In South America?"

"Brazil, to be exact. You ever been there?"

"Oh, no."

"You'd like it. Lots of plants."

"What kind of people do you take through the jungle?"

"Scientists, mostly, out of a little village called Rio Negro. There's tons of environmental research going on down there with saving the rain forests. We're one of the few outfits which have connections with both the government and the natives, so we can get people pretty much wherever they want to go."

"On horseback?" she asked.

"Sometimes. But mostly by boat," he said, and went to offer his hand to Butcher to sniff. The dog growled.

"He's not ready yet. Give him time."

"I know," Zach said, moving back to provide the dog some room. "Bullheaded."

"You have any dogs of your own?"

"Why do you ask?"

"Your way with animals."

"You're not back to that cowboy thing again, are you? And we were having such a pleasant conversation."

He went to refill his mug, then held up the coffeepot in silent question. "No, thank you," she said, smiling a little. "I prefer tea, myself."

He shrugged, returned the pot to the burner and lounged against the counter, studying her. "If you hadn't figured it out yet, I'm not much good at apologizing."

"I can see that."

"You're not going to make this easy for me, are you?"

A grin played around his mouth. Yet in his eyes she saw a guarded expression that made her recall the house. Rather than answer the question, she went to the pack she'd left by the door and pulled out the first thing she'd bought after she left the Community, a dog's plastic dish. "Butcher's bowl," she said, giving it to him.

"Thanks," he said, and added, "In more ways than one."

A curious warmth ran through her veins, the warmth of an acknowledgment both heartfelt and freely bestowed. Suddenly it no longer mattered that he wasn't the most eloquent of men. "You're welcome."

She watched while he crumpled the dog treats into bite-size pieces and set the bowl on the floor. "Here, boy."

Butcher ignored the command. She didn't interfere, wanting to know how Zach would handle the situation. He knelt on the floor and waited patiently, allowing the dog to set the pace. When Butcher at last ambled over, Zach didn't try to pet him but held the bowl so the dog could get every crumb. It was a gesture of faith, one that was rewarded when Butcher finished and sniffed at Zach's fingers. He scratched the dog's chin and Butcher tentatively wagged his tail. Working his way behind the dog's ears, Zach petted the animal with long strokes. His hands were large and brown, and, she remembered, very strong. "Coburn tells me you're looking for a job," he said at last.

"Yes," she said, and tore her gaze away. She took a deep breath. "I wish to pay off my debt to you."

That got his attention. "*Your* debt?"

"I want to buy your house."

"I don't have a house."

"The main house, over yonder, on the other side of the trees."

He left off making nice to the dog and stood. "You've got to be kidding," he said, washing his hands. "No one's lived in that place for years. Besides, it's part of the ranch. I can't sell one without the other."

She handed him the towel she'd been knotting in her hands. "Then I'd like to purchase the entire ranch."

"Excuse me?"

"The ranch. I'd like to purchase it."

"With what? Your good looks?"

"With the ten thousand dollars you offered me yesterday."

There was a prolonged silence. "I don't know where you went to school, lady, but the arithmetic doesn't add up. The land alone is worth at least fifty times that."

"That's why I need a job."

"Oh, yeah. Your logic is faultless."

"Are you turning down my offer?"

"Believe it or not."

"Then I have an alternate suggestion. Allow me to live in the house and help you get it ready to sell."

"In return for what? A million dollars?"

She looked at him straight on, dead serious. "The price of repairs. As you said, no one has lived there for years. It's pretty run-down."

The barest gleam of humor lit his eyes. "Did Coburn put you up to this?"

"No. However, when I mentioned it, he said you might show some resistance to a request to stay in the house. He said you boarded it up yourself after your father died."

Zach glanced at the door. "What else did he tell you?"

"Nothing more," she said carefully. "He is, above all else, a loyal man."

"Yes, he is." Zach turned back, eyeing her speculatively. "You could just pull in your marker. I'm the one who owes you, remember?"

"All you owe me is a chemise and a pair of shoes."

Reminded, Zach glanced down. Her feet peeked out from beneath her skirt, ten toes of bare accusation. Yet accusations were the last thing she'd given him this morning.

His gaze traveled up the length of brown skirt and took in the faded clay color of her calico blouse. The entire effect was monochromatic, steeped in sepia tones, like that of an old tintype photograph. And it wasn't just the clothes that harkened back to an earlier time, a different era. Her scrubbed skin, bound hair, and direct manner were equally old-fashioned, commanding a respect he wasn't quite ready to deliver. Not when it was so foreign to his experience.

"Why do I get the feeling you're totally out of your depth here?" he asked.

"Oh, but I'm not," she said, giving him the full effect of her most dazzling smile. "You are."

Five

Sarah could tell her answer didn't sit well with him. He frowned at her and she experienced the sensation of standing on very thin ice.

"Feeling a little feisty, are we?" he asked.

"Feisty is one word for it." Foolhardy was another. She hadn't forgotten his strength, or his mercurial moods. But she fancied she knew what lay behind them. "So, have you had time enough to consider the matter? Will you hire me?"

Zach shrugged, trying to gauge precisely what was most important to her, the house or the job. When it came to Sarah, he could use the leverage. "In exchange for cooking two meals a day and keeping the common areas of the bunkhouse reasonably clean, I'll give you room, board, and two hundred dollars a week."

"Agreed. And the house?"

"I'll think about it."

"I may not have much of a head for business, but I do know it will be difficult to sell in its present condition."

"If someone wants the land badly enough, they won't care. Years ago, I thought about razing the house myself."

She looked horrified. "Whatever for?"

"It belonged to my father. He and I didn't get along."

"What about your mother?"

"She left when I was eight. Divorce."

"Nevertheless, the house is extremely well built. It's stood the test of time. I know it must be worth something."

"Possibly."

"Surely you'll get a higher price for the land if all buildings are in good condition, will you not?"

"I told you. I'll think about it."

"Is that not why you've engaged the hands to stay on for another month?"

"Enough, Sarah. I meant what I said—I'll think about it. Now, we've got some other business to take care of. Come on." He grabbed the keys to the pickup from a set of hooks next to the door.

"Where are we going?"

"Shopping, remember? A new chemise and pair of shoes coming right up."

Zach's plan was to take her to the nearest discount department store, pay her enough money to cover the underwear and sneakers, then give her an advance on her salary so she could get everything else she so obviously needed. Shopping was a chore for him and he wanted to get it over with in the shortest amount of time possible. But as he drove, he reconsidered his destination. He didn't want to look cheap, and there was no law that said he had to replace her stuff with exactly the same thing—if she could even find the same thing. In fact, it would be smart to insist she accept a good dose of his generosity to balance everything out. So he drove the extra miles to Crossroads Mall and herded her into Amsterdam's, the most expensive department store in town.

Their first stop was the credit department. He had to take her hand to lead her there because, from the moment they walked through the elegant heavy-glass entrance doors, she was distracted.

"I know you can't wait to get on with your shopping, but I need to set you up with a card you can use on your own," he said, ushering her to the customer service window.

He opened an account under his name and put her down as a cosigner. When he handed her the pen and she wrote her signature, her hand shook, and he recalled her stumbling over Smith when she'd first told him her name. "Don't worry," he said. "As long as I pay the bills, it's all legal."

She nodded but he could tell by the way she rubbed her temples she was still worried.

"You'll feel a lot better once you buy yourself some new clothes." He pressed the temporary card into her hand and walked her back to the main aisle. "I'll meet you at the entrance where we came in," he said, and consulted his watch. "Say, in two hours. That should give you plenty of time."

"You're leaving me here?"

Zach realized it was the first time she'd said a word since they'd left the ranch. "I've got a few things I need to buy, too," he said. "We'll get out of here a lot faster if we split up."

"But what if something should go wrong?" She stared at the card in her hand as though it were a foreign object.

"What could go wrong? The card has a credit limit, so I know you can't go too crazy." She looked at him and he saw the sheen of tears in her eyes. What in the world was her problem?

"I'd hoped we would remain together," she said.

"We'll be together later. By the time the two hours are up, it'll be time to eat. We'll go out for lunch," he offered, figuring that would appease her.

She caught his arm. "Zach, please. I don't know what I'm supposed to do."

She gestured in dismay at the nearest display, which happened to be two mannequins posed in skimpy silk robes. Zach couldn't help but wonder what she would look like wearing one of them. "Look," he said. "They have a huge selection. If you check it out, I'm sure you'll be able to find something you like. Now, I've got to go."

"But I've never done this."

"Never done what?"

"Bought things like this."

"Come on, Sarah. It's just like buying things anywhere else," he said, showing his impatience. Good grief, the woman acted like she'd never been in a store before. "You see something you like and take it to the cash register. Show the salesperson this card and he or she will take it from there, believe me."

"That's all?"

"That's all."

He left her standing in front of the robe display and cut through the dress department. Clingy women always gave him the creeps and Sarah's helplessness made him feel even more irritated than usual. Up to now, she hadn't seemed like the type.

He glanced over his shoulder, hoping that she'd found solace in an armload of clothes. She stood unmoving where he had left her, smack-dab in the middle of the aisle, her fingers pleating the folds of her skirt. He ducked behind a set of mannequins. Through the crook of a stiffly bent arm, he watched another shopper, laden with packages and towing two children, pass Sarah by, forcing her to step aside or be trampled.

The jar into reality broke her reverie. She visibly swallowed and her hand splayed across the bodice of her blouse. Squaring her shoulders, she looked all around. The ceiling seemed to hold particular fascination.

Zach followed her gaze upward. Sprinkler heads, fluorescent lights and the occasional built-in speaker blasting instrumental music. Nothing out of the ordinary.

She reached out to touch the silk robe hanging on the display. Her hand barely grazed a sleeve before she sprang back as though bitten. Retreating, she collided with a rack of dresses across the aisle. Some fell, the hangers clattering on the marble floor. She quickly knelt and scooped them up, checking to see if anyone was looking. Fortunately it was a weekday morning and there were few shoppers.

She juggled the hangers, trying to get them back on the rack. Sympathy tightened his gut. For whatever reason, this was all new to her. The bright lights, the variety of colors and textures, the sheer volume of merchandise was overwhelming her.

He retraced his steps, unsure of what he might say, especially after his earlier brush-off. He tapped her shoulder and she turned around, wearing the same expression he remembered from yesterday. Wary. A woman alone.

"Come on," he said. "I'll get you started."

Her hand felt small and clammy within his. He tucked it within the shelter of his arm and led her to the back of the lingerie section. Two salesladies were talking behind the cash register. He picked the older one, a straightlaced, gray-haired matronly type, hoping her age would help Sarah feel more comfortable and cut down on the time this little rescue mission might take. "Excuse me, ma'am," he said. "I have a young lady here who needs your help."

"Yes, sir."

"This is Sarah. Sarah, this is Ms..."

"Mrs. Schwartz."

"Mrs. Schwartz," he continued, approving of her formal demeanor. "You should know that Sarah recently returned from a trip overseas. Now that she's back in the States, she needs all new lingerie."

"Well, you've certainly come to the right place, my dear. Your size?"

Zach saw Sarah's blank reaction, and said, "I think you'll need to measure her yourself, Mrs. Schwartz. It's been a while."

"Of course. Come with me, dear."

"Zach?" Sarah asked.

"It's okay," he said, squeezing her hand. "Mrs. Schwartz will take you into the fitting room to find out how...uh, big you are. I'll wait right here."

They returned a few minutes later. The saleslady looked pleased while Sarah looked scandalized.

"Thirty-two C and a perfect size six," Mrs. Schwartz announced.

Zach frowned, annoyed that she found it necessary to broadcast Sarah's measurements for anyone to hear. Luckily there were no other customers in the department. "She'll need everything," he said curtly. "From top to bottom."

The two salesladies bustled around, gathering different styles of bras, panties, slips and camisoles.

Sarah leaned close to him and spoke in a low tone. "Zach, it is not acceptable for a man to buy a woman of short acquaintance these kinds of clothes."

"Sarah, you lost your chemise and shoes because of me. I'm simply replacing them."

"You will be buying much more than I lost."

"You're going to be working for me. It's important that everyone who is employed at the ranch wear good clothes that will last."

"But I can never repay you, even if I worked for you a very long time."

He pulled her away from the curious stares of the salesladies. "Sarah, I will only say this once. You need to wear regular clothes, especially underneath. Did you know everything you have is so worn, it's practically transparent? For my own sanity, allow me to get these things for you."

Her cheeks pinkened and she stopped arguing. When they returned to the cash register, she meekly followed the bustling Mrs. Schwartz into the fitting rooms. Zach settled into a chair outside. He'd stay long enough to make sure Sarah was okay, then take off.

Mrs. Schwartz emerged two minutes later with a definite frown on her face. "Come with me, young man."

"What's wrong?" he asked with a sigh. At this rate he'd be here all day.

"The young lady absolutely refuses to cooperate. She won't even answer my questions."

The old biddy sounded so put out, Zach didn't bother to reply. She was beginning to get on his nerves. Maybe Sarah felt the same way.

He followed the helmet of gray hair into the fitting room entrance and halted. Had Sarah felt the same suffocation he did when confronted by the overblown glamour of each thickly carpeted cubicle? Framed brass floor-length mirrors covered opposing walls and the delicate peach-colored chairs scattered around didn't look as if they could support a cat much less a human being. One louvered door was closed.

Mrs. Schwartz pointed to it, stage-whispering, "She says she doesn't believe such clumsily made things can cost so much. She refuses to let me help her try on anything until I went to get you. She told me she wants you to see, and I quote, 'How little your money is buying.' Just how many years did she spend overseas, anyway?"

"I'll take care of it," Zach said.

"Please see that you do. I'll be out by the register, guarding the fitting room entrance. I certainly wouldn't want any of our customers coming in here and finding a *man*."

"No, we certainly wouldn't want that," Zach said, struggling to rein in his temper. He waited until Mrs. Schwartz disappeared from view before knocking on Sarah's door.

"It's me," he said.

"Oh, thank God." He heard her draw the bolt back on the lock. Zach caught the knob of the door and held it closed.

"Just tell me what the problem is, Sarah."

"Is the mistress gone?"

The *mistress?* "Yeah, I think so."

"I have to show you these undergarments and I don't want anyone else to see."

"Well, if that's the case, I don't think you should be showing me, either."

"Yesterday I was wearing less than what I have on right now."

That put an interesting picture in his head. "Sarah, I shouldn't be in here. This dressing room is for women only. Mrs. Schwartz should be helping you, not me."

"I don't like her."

"I'll get the other saleslady, then."

"I don't want anyone else. You told me you could see right through my clothes. So what do you think would happen if I wore this?"

A wispy bra slipped through the louvers and fluttered to the floor. Zach bent to pick it up.

Sarah opened the door, wearing an expression of indignation. She also wore a floor-length flannel robe that hid most of her body, a fact Zach was extremely thankful for. He held up the bra, dangling it by a thin strap. "If you want something a bit more substantial, all you have to do is ask."

"What I want is a corset and a cotton chemise to wear underneath it. When I asked Mrs. Schwartz to bring me one of each, she laughed at me."

"Well, she shouldn't have done that," Zach said, trying to imagine the staid saleslady laughing. The image wouldn't come. Instead he remembered her pinched mouth, so full of judgment. "Sarah, listen. I know you're not used to these things." He disentangled the straps from the lace cups and held the bra up. "I know they look strange, compared to, uh, a corset. But I think you'll find that this will work just as well as what you're used to."

"Men don't wear these things, do they?"

"No, but I know what I'm talking about," he said, thinking about the wide variety of bras he'd unfastened in his life.

"How?"

"I have a mother and two sisters."

"Sisters? You do?"

"I do."

"It's hard for me to think of you as being part of a regular family. They don't live on the ranch?"

"When my parents divorced, my dad got custody of the boys and my mom got custody of the girls. She moved to Florida and I haven't seen her or my sisters since." He pushed the bra back into her hands. "Now, get going, Sarah. I'd like to be out of here before the end of the next century."

She put her hand on top of his, preventing him from closing the door. "Your family was split in two?"

"Believe me, it was better that way." He backed out of the cubicle. "I'll see you out by the cash register when you're finished."

"How many brothers do you have?"

"Two." He reached to close the door.

"Their names?"

"Come on, Sarah," he scolded. "We'll talk later, okay? After you're finished."

"Talk to me now while I figure out how to put this on."

His lascivious thoughts must have shown on his face because she wagged a finger at him. "I meant for you to talk to me from there," she said, indicating a spindly chair just outside her fitting room.

"I told you—women only."

''Why does it matter? You and I are the only ones here.''

Precisely, he wanted to say.

''Please, Zach. Talking will make me feel less addle-pated.''

''Addlepated?''

''You can tell, can't you? Everyone can tell just by look-ing at me how ignorant I am.''

''So you've never worn a bra before. That doesn't make you ignorant.''

''I don't know how to put them on.''

''I'll get the saleslady to help you.''

''She'll laugh at me again, especially when she sees that I don't know what I'm doing. Stay with me, Zach. Please.''

''If you promise to try this stuff on right now, as fast as you can, I'll wait out here.''

He pulled the door shut and briefly glanced at the chair before settling on the floor with his back against the wall opposite Sarah's dressing room. He stretched out and crossed his legs at the ankles, vaguely noting the bare feet just beyond the pointy toes of his cowboy boots.

His focus abruptly sharpened. Her toes, her feet, her calves were all visible under the bottom of the door. Fortu-nately, he thought cynically—or unfortunately, depending on his point of view—the little louvers were going the wrong way, so even at this low angle, he couldn't see her body. But the bottom ten inches of her legs he had a tremendous view of, thank you very much.

''Well?'' she asked. Her right foot lifted and disap-peared, then came down and flattened on the plush gray carpet. Her left foot rose...

''Well what?''

And joined its twin a moment later. Her heels came off the floor and she went up on her toes, turning this way and that. The soles of her feet looked a lot better than yester-day. The scratches underneath were healing up nicely.

"The names." A scrap of pink nylon fell down to her ankles and she stepped out of the skimpy briefs.

"What?" He leaned his head back and stared at the ceiling, his mouth dry.

"You said you had two sisters and two brothers. What are their names?"

"First, there's Abraham," he said, trying to think. The ceiling wasn't helping, either.

"Then?"

"Uh...Elizabeth." He couldn't stand it anymore. He looked. She was stepping into a pool of ivory satin.

"Then?"

"Joseph."

"And your other sister?" Her hands reached down and pulled up the satin.

The satin whisked up her legs, becoming a slip with a creamy lace hem. "Lacy," he said.

"What kind of name is that?"

The hem settled around the tops of her calves, caressing them. "Margaret," he said. "Her name is Margaret."

"All biblical," she said.

"Come again?"

"All the names in your family come from the Bible. We do the same."

There was a rustling sound. She must be trying something on over the slip. He picked up the thread of the conversation, vowing to keep his mind on asking her some questions, even if it killed him. "We?"

"My people."

"What kind of people?"

"The people of the Community."

"Is that the name of your hometown?"

"It's what we call it. Officially we are known as the Community Order."

"Sounds like a religious cult."

"It is not the same as those I have read about in the newspapers. There is no talk of an imminent Armageddon, or the stockpiling of many weapons. Indeed, the Community was founded on the principles of harmony, spirituality and simplicity. We live much as farmers and ranchers did a hundred years ago."

"You mean, like the Amish?"

"Yes, my mother told me of the Old Orders. We, too, live a plain life, although only some follow a literal translation of the Bible. Those who founded the Community came from many different traditions. My father told me how, thirty years ago, many young people of his generation chose to return to the ways of the forefathers. The Community was founded to celebrate such a life."

"You mean, the Community is not part of an organized religious group?"

"Correct. My father, for example, grew up on a reservation and believed in the concept of a Great Spirit. My mother, on the other hand, was raised in a Christian home and had me baptized in Jesus' name."

"What did you end up believing in?"

"My beliefs combine both, actually. In my mind, the Great Spirit is another name for God, the Creator of us all."

Zach nodded, amazed that with all the religious dogma she spouted, he shared similar beliefs.

The door opened. "Is this really supposed to hang from my shoulders so?"

She wore the satin slip and a matching camisole, with the bra in the right place underneath. But the straps were loose and fell down over her slender upper arms. Zach scrambled to his feet. "Not unless you're Madonna."

"Certainly if bras are a modern invention, the Madonna would not have dressed in such a fashion."

"I was talking about a different Madonna," he said, beginning to understand the limits of Sarah's experience. No wonder she acted wise one minute and dumb the next. She had very little knowledge of modern day life. "She's a pop singer."

Her nose wrinkled. "A what kind of singer?"

"A singer who is very popular nowadays. She's a bit more free with her clothes than either you or the Virgin Mary. There," he said, tightening the straps. "How does that feel?"

"Strange."

"Well, it looks..." He tried not to leer. "Great."

"And one is supposed to wear this under every piece of clothing?"

"At night you can go free. I mean, when you're sleeping, you don't wear anything. That is to say—"

"You don't have to be embarrassed, Zach. Women of the Community don't wear their corsets at night, either."

He chuckled, appreciating the irony of having Sarah, dressed in little more than a few scraps of satin, tell him not to be embarrassed. For the next hour he tightened straps, undid hooks, and generally made himself useful while she chattered away like a magpie. He learned she'd grown up an only child, and had been educated along with the other children of the Community in a one-room school. When she was fifteen, her father died in a tractor accident. Her mother had hired a man named Cal to help with the work and, within a year, had married him. Sarah claimed she'd never liked him, but her mother was sick. Sarah had stayed on under Cal's roof for several years to care for her mother. When she died, Sarah had left the Community, simple as that, saying she had wanted to see something of how other people lived.

Approving her sense of adventure, Zach wasn't much better in the long story department, telling her about some of the places he'd visited during his many years of traveling the world. After they left the dressing room and waited in front of the cash register for Mrs. Schwartz to add up the tally, he timed his best confession for last, launching into a story from childhood about how he used to raid his sisters' panty drawers to make parachutes for his plastic army men.

Mrs. Schwartz looked suitably appalled.

He and Sarah were walking away, shopping bags in hand, when Sarah asked what a parachute was. He described the equipment needed for jumping out of airplanes in such detail she asked if he had ever jumped out of an airplane himself.

"Among other things."

"Weren't you scared?" she asked, her eyes wide. "I have seen airplanes flying in the sky overhead. They are up so high."

"Sure it's high. But that's half the fun, the adrenaline rush."

"What is an 'adrenaline rush'?"

He ushered her to the main aisle and tried to explain the compulsion that drove him to climb the tallest mountains and sail the stormiest seas, searching for the ultimate adventure. "For now it's in Brazil, deep in the last true virgin jungle on earth," he said at the end of his little lecture. "After that, I'll head south as far as I can go—to Antarctica. It's the only continent I haven't been on."

"I know from my geography lessons how cold and inhospitable Antarctica is," she said with a shiver. "Do you not get tired of traveling? Do you not want to find a place to call your own and settle down?"

"I like my freedom."

"Freedom from what?"

She really didn't get it. Talking to someone as naive as Sarah was like talking to his government suppliers in Brazil. In translating English to Portuguese, he had to formulate his thoughts very clearly to communicate effectively. He thought for a moment, struggling to define his philosophy of life in one word. "Responsibility."

"You have no desire to be responsible?"

"Only for myself."

"What about your family, your brothers and sisters?"

"My older brother, Bram, has stayed in touch, but all I have in common with the rest is the same last name."

"Surely you could create a new family, one of your own choosing. What about marriage and children?"

How typical for a woman like Sarah to think along those lines. "What do I want a wife and children for? They would only get in my way. I like my life just the way it is."

Puzzlement creased her brow. "Are you one of those happy men who don't like closets?"

Happy? Closets? The confusion in her tone was his final clue. Comprehension dawned. Under most circumstances, he would have been offended at the conclusion she'd drawn. But with Sarah, he halted in the middle of the aisle, laughing outright. "You think I'm gay?"

"Yes, that's the word. I've been reading about it in magazines and newspapers. I understand it is quite the thing nowadays. You've already told me how much you enjoy being on the cutting blade."

"Edge, Sarah. I think you mean cutting 'edge.'"

"Of course. Edge. How silly of me."

Flustered by her mistake, her cheeks took on a rosy blush. That and the assumption she'd made caused him to decide he needed to set her straight, pun very much intended. He glanced around the store and saw the coast was clear. "I am not gay, Sarah."

"You're not?" she asked, obviously confused.

"You want to know how I'm absolutely, positively sure?" He curled a finger under her chin and looked at her mouth.

She must have had an inkling she was in way over her head because she licked her lips in that nervous way he recognized. "I have a confession to make, Zach."

"Really?"

"Yes. You see, I don't exactly know, in this particular context, what the word gay means. The newspapers didn't explain it very well and when I looked it up in the dictionary, the definition didn't make a great deal of sense.''

"I bet. Would you like me to give you a clear definition?''

She nodded.

"To understand, you have to stay very still. Promise?''

"Why should I have to stay still?''

"Because,'' he said, "I'm going to kiss you like you've never been kissed before.''

Six

"Kiss me? Here? Why?"

Her last question was edged in panic and Sarah put up her hands to push him away. But he had hold of her chin and his other hand was curving around the back of her neck, pulling her close.

Unlike yesterday, his fingers weren't punishing and he wore the funniest smile. At once bemused and tender, it tugged at her, and she felt herself drawn in.

At first his lips barely touched hers. His taste teased; she could smell mint and freshness of the breeze from this morning that had lifted his hair. The palm she had flattened against his chest picked up his heartbeat. The same rapid rhythm drummed in her own ears. The gentleness of his mouth was a marked contrast. Perhaps that was what made her lean into him—the novelty of his gentleness.

He spread his hand downward from her chin and across the exposed arch of her neck. She knew she was lost when the threat she should have felt wasn't there. Even when the kiss deepened and his thumb caressed the base of her throat, her instinct for self-preservation remained utterly quiet. Instead she felt the sweet rush of anticipation.

"Open up for me, Sarah," he whispered.

She had no idea what he meant until he nudged the line of her mouth with his tongue and shivers raced down her spine. Her knees unlocked. She was falling, spinning, had to hold on to something. The hand on his chest fisted and gripped the loose front of his shirt.

My God, she thought. Save me.

Zach felt her sway and grabbed her arms, breaking the kiss. He'd barely touched her, yet she looked at him with dazed eyes, two high spots of color on her cheeks. He grinned, ignoring a sudden wish to kiss her again. One appeared to be quite enough.

"Not gay. Got that, Sarah?"

She put her hands to her cheeks in confusion. "You're not happy because you kissed me?"

Her naiveté had the most perverse effect on him. Chuckling, he whispered a clear definition in her ear. Even with the barest of clinical details, color flooded her face.

Drawing back, she stared at him, unable to disguise her shock. "But how?"

"I'll leave that up to your imagination," he said.

She blushed to the roots of her hair. It was then he vowed to teach her more than how to kiss—debts, obligations and employment contracts be damned. He would find a way. Sarah was much too innocent for her own good.

Taking her hand, he led her on a detour through the women's sportswear department. She was so nonplussed by their conversation, she didn't utter a word of protest. He was able to flag down another saleslady, a much younger one this time, and asked her to pick out some everyday clothes for a young woman of twenty-four who wore a perfect size six.

The woman seemed to understand Sarah's taste with one look, for she returned with a dozen outfits fashioned, as she said, in retro-style. A half hour later Sarah was wearing a flowing burgundy dress that ended in a swirl around her knees. It was modest yet elegant, and fit her so perfectly he bought another one just like it in blue. He also bought two skirts, five blouses and three pairs of jeans, even though she claimed she'd never wear them.

"We'll see," he said.

If she'd been uncharacteristically quiet about the clothes, she was the opposite when they finally made it to the shoe department. Though she mispronounced the brand name Nike to rhyme with mike, she rattled off her size and favorite style in record time. When he pointed out possible footwear to go with her new dress, the latest in platform shoes made her shake her head in dismay. They finally settled on the sneakers, some low-heeled, navy leather pumps and a pair of fleece-lined slippers he picked out himself. Winter was approaching and he remembered how cold those wood floors in the old house could be.

He caught himself. *Trailer,* he thought. The floor in the trailer could be pretty cold, too.

Their last stop was the hosiery department, where he bought a dozen athletic socks, panty hose and knee-highs. They were strolling toward the exit, both laden with packages, when she stopped to gaze in wonder at the many cosmetic aisles.

Feeling indulgent, he said, "I'll take all the stuff we bought out to the truck while you look around here for a few minutes. When I come back, we'll go to lunch."

She handed over her bags and he set off, feeling like a pack animal. A pretty content pack animal, he decided. So he'd gone over his initial target time. Three hours was pretty good considering everything they'd accomplished.

He loaded the truck and returned to the cosmetic section. He found Sarah immediately, close to the place he'd left her. She hadn't gone very far because she was like a kid in a candy store, picking up the tiny glass bottles, sniffing at various fragrances, pausing to rub lotion between reverent fingers. With the bulk of their shopping done, he was in a hurry to eat, and he placed his hand in the small of her back, urging her along. "Come on, Sarah."

"Wait, Zach. You have to smell this."

She held out the stopper from a diamond-shaped bottle. He dutifully sniffed. The fragrance was delicate, like wildflowers.

A cosmetologist in a white lab coat approached. "May I help you?" she asked.

"Just looking," Zach answered, hoping the woman would take the hint and leave them alone.

"How about you, ma'am?" She smiled at Sarah, showing all her shiny white teeth. Zach noticed her name tag said Mystee, and rolled his eyes.

"We have a special promotion this week," she said. "Would you care for a free facial?"

"This service costs nothing?" Sarah asked, obviously intrigued.

"Sarah, believe me," Zach said, taking her arm. "It may not cost anything up front, but you can bet by the time you're done, you will have shelled out plenty."

"Now, sir," said Mystee, "there is never any obligation to buy."

Sarah turned to him. "May I, Zach?"

Zach groaned inwardly. "We've been shopping for over three hours. It's past one o'clock. Aren't you hungry?"

She reluctantly put down a miniature soap sample.

"It will only take a moment," said Mystee. "We have some wonderful products designed to make skin feel new again. Like this mineral water spray." She spritzed Sarah's forearm.

Zach caught a whiff of the subtle fragrance. It smelled fresh, like the yucca Sarah had used on her hair.

"Surely we can spare a moment, Zach?"

Zach had a feeling any cosmetics the indefatigable Mystee might apply would take considerably more than a moment. The woman was so perfectly made up, her face resembled a mannequin's. "Maybe later," he said. Sarah laid a hand on his arm. "Please?"

"All right," he growled. "But none of that makeup stuff."

"She has such beautiful skin, she really doesn't need any." Mystee led Sarah to a padded stool behind the counter. "And I can assure you, ma'am, you always will have beautiful skin if you follow our simple five-step, complexion-care regimen."

The simple five-step, complexion-care regimen took twenty minutes to apply. First came scrub cream, then cleansing lotion, a pink-tinted refreshener, then a spritz with the mineral spray, and finally a moisturizer, complete with sunscreen. But Zach couldn't begrudge Sarah the time as he watched her sit and be pampered. Had anyone ever fussed over her before? Seeing the absolute bliss on her face, he doubted it.

When the cosmetologist picked up one of those eyeliner pencils, Zach did interfere. "I said, no makeup."

"You're absolutely right. Her complexion is so fine, she doesn't need any foundation," Mystee said smoothly. "I'm just going to play up her eyes a little bit," she added, already sketching under Sarah's lower lashes. "Such dark eyes deserve a bit of highlighting. A little color will bring them right out. And, of course, lip gloss never hurt anyone."

He kept his mouth shut for the extra five minutes, which was more than plenty, because his heart stopped when Sarah slid off the chair. It wasn't so much the burgundy dress, or the makeup, either. It was the glow in her eyes.

"You like it, Zach?"

He liked it too much. "Very nice."

"No one will laugh at me now."

He ended up buying a couple of the products, just to see her light up again. Then he took her to a restaurant inside the mall, a nice sit-down place. After the hostess seated them, Sarah perched on the edge of her chair, supremely self-conscious, judging by the surreptitious looks she cast at the other diners.

"Yes, they're all looking at you," Zach said.

"They are?"

"The women are all looking because they're jealous of you. The men are all looking because they're jealous of me."

She laughed and called him a terrible liar, but the compliment must have hit home because she focused on the menu, concentrating on it with the same single-minded zeal with which she approached everything. He found he liked that about her, though he couldn't exactly say why. Her single-mindedness could also be a big pain in the butt.

The waitress came by. Sarah ordered a hamburger, fries, and a glass of milk, the last of which made him smile. He said he'd take the same, but substituted a bottle of beer for the milk. There was only so much clean living he could take.

"Well," he said after the waitress left. "Are you having a good time?"

"Oh, yes." Her eyes fairly danced. "Are you?"

"I hate shopping," he said, and took her hand to soften the bluntness of the admittance. "But I'll go with you again anytime."

"You mean that?"

"One thing you should know about me, Sarah. When I say something, I mean it."

"That brings to mind a discussion we had earlier today."

"What discussion was that?" he asked, wondering which figured higher on her list: the wonders of modern lingerie, adrenaline rushes, or homosexuality.

"You must have had plenty of time to think while I was trying on all those clothes. What about the house?"

* * *

She wore him down. There was no other explanation.

Zach decided this on the way back to the Bar M late that afternoon. With Sarah perched on the seat next to him in the truck, surrounded by shopping bags, he realized how, slowly but surely, she had actually gotten him to reconsider one of the most solemn promises he'd ever made to himself.

It wasn't her badgering that made him rethink his stand concerning the house. It was her sense of excitement about the prospect of moving in, the way she gestured and talked with light in her eyes, explaining what she would do and how she planned to fix it up if he allowed her to live there.

He liked how confident she was, how sure of herself. Even when she'd felt overwhelmed in the store, her natural optimism and poise had quickly reasserted itself, once she'd gotten used to the pretensions of the surroundings. Considering her background, he thought she'd be different—meek and mild, or more judgmental—given her spouting from the Good Book. But though her beliefs were strong, they were tempered by a pragmatism that came from thinking for herself. Sarah was definitely not close-minded. And neither, Zach decided, was he. So how could he justify saying no to such a simple request?

Ten years ago, on the day of his father's funeral, he'd gone through and boarded up the house out of spite. Spite for home, for family, for the entire ranching life. Opening the house would mean reopening old wounds—wounds he'd gone out of his way to close. But in listening to Sarah's plans, he couldn't help but see the wisdom of what she proposed. The Bar M would attract higher bids if all the buildings were in good shape. Even better, his debt to Sarah would fully be repaid. Being generous with the clothes was easy—too easy. She had risked more than mere clothes when she dragged him out of the creek. The injuries to her hands and feet attested to that.

Granted, going back on his word went against the grain. Yet there were times a man had to weigh the needs of oth-

ers over those of his own. And though he'd made a career
of rejecting that notion, this was one time he recognized it
was his turn to do a favor. Sarah had certainly done him one
in saving his life. He could compromise on this one thing
and let her do what she wanted. It didn't mean he actually
had to set foot in the place. All he had to do was oversee the
work. He could still insist she serve meals out of the bunkhouse. Being boss did carry some prerogatives.

Over the past couple of years, he'd sometimes wondered
what it would feel like to come home to a woman after a
long, hard day, to look forward to a feeling of welcome and
a good, hot meal. With Sarah, he could test the experience
without risking any loss of autonomy. She knew up front
her job was only temporary, that once the ranch was sold,
they would part company.

He wouldn't have risked such an arrangement, otherwise.

She wore him down. There was no other explanation.

Sarah stood at the back door of the main house, survey-
ing her new domain with pride. She had spent the past week
alone cleaning this one room, a nice, big kitchen. Now the
surfaces gleamed, and every plate, bowl, platter and dish
was washed and put away in an orderly fashion. The odor
of baking bread permeated the air, and on the long, polished dining table, she'd set a ceramic pitcher full of tiny
daisies, found when she'd sheared back the weeds growing
in the garden.

Discovering the daisies had been a pleasant surprise, the
latest in a week of pleasant surprises. The first had been
Zach's agreement to let her live in the house. Ever since their
excursion to the mall, they had become easier with each
other, having become friends. Good friends.

Sarah wiped her hands on the apron fronting her gray
wool dress and peered through the window above the
kitchen sink. From here she could see the top of the barn

over the trees. Zach stood upon the roof, working to fix a gaping hole. He wore what he called his jungle outfit: camouflage fatigues and heavy, thick-soled boots. His bare back attested to the fine autumn day, clear and sunny, with temperatures in the high fifties. After the first snowfall of the season earlier in the week, the weather had been pleasant for several days. Zach had seized the opportunity to repair several of the outbuildings.

The hammer in his hand flashed in the sun. He was tireless, up at dawn and not stopping until well after dusk. Invariably, he already had a pot of coffee going in the machine at the bunkhouse when she arrived at 5:00 a.m. to prepare breakfast.

That had been one of the conditions he'd imposed when he'd agreed to let her live here. *All meals will be served in the bunkhouse.* At the time she thought it a practical suggestion, for the main house's kitchen was far from usable then. But now she knew this was to be a permanent arrangement.

Sarah felt the smile slip from her face. Zach repeatedly refused to come near the house. A not-so-wonderful surprise.

She had tried everything she could think of to get him inside, to show him the improvements taking shape. Oh, he was nice enough about it, treating her with an indulgence he rarely showed to anyone else. He'd hired a plumber and an electrician to make the place safe and immediately livable, and in another week, an army of painters was due to come. But he flatly refused to inspect their handiwork, saying if what they did was fine by her, it was fine by him.

When she asked if the house held unpleasant memories for him, he clammed up completely. So she attempted to learn more about Zach and his family from what was in the house. And especially, from what wasn't in it.

Someone must have liked plants, for there were clay pots in all the rooms, in every nook and cranny. She couldn't afford to buy the greenery to fill them all, so she started with cuttings from the garden and planted seeds from some packets she had found in a kitchen drawer.

The volumes of books crammed on every shelf were more problematic. Most were paperbacks, and so old the pages crumbled when she opened them. The hardcovers she cleaned meticulously, marveling over the inscriptions she often found inside. At one time Zach's father had loved Zach's mother enough to indulge her apparent passion for books.

On the other hand, there weren't any photographs. Photographs of family, of the ranch, of anything. During her journey, she'd become accustomed to the visual aspects of modern society, how images were everywhere. Newspapers, magazines, television, motion pictures—everywhere she turned there were photographs, pieces of life frozen in time. And this house didn't have one, not even a calendar.

Sarah turned her attention to the potatoes drying in the sink and began to peel, letting her thoughts wander. Tomorrow she would tackle the front room. It needed a good airing, and half the furniture had to go since she'd found several mouse nests in the upholstery. Then there was the big master bedroom upstairs where she and Butcher slept. She'd done nothing there but air the large mattress and wash the sheets. And there were still the four other upstairs bedrooms. So far, she hadn't the time to do anything more than glance at them.

Why wouldn't Zach come near the house?

Sarah watched Zach move with precision on the roof across the yard and put her hand against the windowpane. She felt its solid warmth against her palm. It reminded her of the time he had kissed her, really kissed her. She had placed her hand on his chest and felt his heart pound. Just as hers was pounding now.

She would go see him, she decided. She had worn him down once. She could do it again.

Seven

From his vantage point on the roof, Zach saw Sarah come out of the house carrying a tray complete with a pitcher and two drinking glasses. Uh-oh, he thought wryly. Another bribe.

As always, Butcher followed at her heels. Playfully barking, he pretended to attack the rippling hem of her skirt. She still insisted on wearing her old clothes, saying there was no use in throwing good after bad when cleaning out years of dirt. Today she wore the calico blouse and the long, brown skirt, covered by a white apron. As usual, her hair was coiled at the back of her head, showing off her graceful neck.

The neck he'd wanted to strangle more than once these past two weeks.

She was driving him crazy. He hadn't abandoned his plan to seduce her, although he was taking more time than he usually did on courtship rituals. This was a campaign, after all, and campaigns required the occasional concession. But she was just as bent on having her way with him, and her campaign involved a different type of seduction.

Every day, she wanted to show him something of what she was doing. Every day, she invited him into the house.

She was so earnest about it, proud of her progress, brimming with excitement. He always politely refused, having no desire to revisit the place he associated with the worst years of his life. Besides, he told her, the house was going to be sold soon.

"To me?" she'd ask, grinning.

He always chuckled, appreciating the teasing glint in her eyes. Not long ago, she hadn't been able to trust him enough to show such good humor. But inside he was struggling between his wishes and hers, and the desire of a man obsessed.

He wanted her. By God, he wanted her. And a disagreement about the house was not going to stop him from having her.

Since he knew Sarah would not be easily persuaded to his bed, he sought her out at odd times of the day, just to ensure they could be alone and have time to get to know one another. He made himself indispensable, driving her to the grocery store for supplies, to the library for books, and to the bank to deposit her paycheck in the savings account he'd helped her open. At night, in the mellow hour or two after supper but before turn-in time, they often watched videos on TV or played cards.

Not the hottest way to seduce a woman, but what else could he do? Pounce when she least expected? He'd tried that already and look what it got him. A live-in ranch housekeeper who made him wish he could stay stateside for a few more weeks. Make that months.

She turned every negative into a positive. The men raved about her cooking. She worked like a demon in the garden, harvesting what was edible and clearing the rest away. She even applied mulch to encourage stuff to grow again next year.

She'd strung up a new clothesline on the aluminum posts on the south side of the house and every sunny morning freshly washed linens appeared on it, flapping in the fall breeze. From the day the electrician had restored power to the house, baking smells had drifted across the yard. Fresh muffins appeared on the breakfast table and she served the crustiest bread this side of San Francisco. For dessert after supper, there were pies, cookies, cakes. The men had never been so well fed.

And he had never felt so starved.

With a vigor that matched hers, he threw himself into the work of preparing the place to sell, telling her in every way he knew how that all her work would be for naught. And still she asked him to see the results of it, hope in her eyes. She was going to ask again, here and now, and he wanted it to stop. Needed it to stop. And there was one sure way Zach knew of to make it stop other than make a blatantly indecent proposal.

He ducked out of her sight and slid down the shingles to the gutter. Butcher would be his biggest problem. The dog still treated him with suspicion, even when Sarah wasn't around. Why Butcher continued to be slow to warm up, Zach didn't bother to guess, but he wasn't above using that to his advantage in getting Sarah off by herself.

When she entered the barnyard, he made the jump from roof to ground in one leap, landing on his feet right in front of her.

"Oh," she said, nearly dropping the tray. "You frightened me."

Butcher barked, but Zach was already standing next to Sarah. "That for me?" he asked, reaching for a glass.

"Hush, Butcher. Yes. Lemonade. I thought you might be thirsty."

"You thought right." Making sure he touched her fingers, he made a show of pouring lemonade from pitcher to glass. Watching her steadily while he drank, he gulped quickly so that some of the liquid spilled and sluiced down his chin and neck. She looked down, obviously flustered.

"I have something to show you in the barn," he said. When she glanced at him, he wiped his bare arm across his mouth and gestured toward the barn door with his lemonade glass.

She put down the tray on a nearby hay bale. Butcher tried to follow her inside and Zach jerked his thumb. "Get lost."

"Close the door after us," she said. "Then he'll stay outside."

He did, making sure that it remained unlatched. He didn't want to scare her too badly.

"What did you want to show me?" she asked. She stood in the middle of the concrete floor, looking around.

He jiggled his glass so the ice inside it clinked loudly. "I fixed the hole in the roof."

She smiled a little. "I saw it from the outside. You did a most wonderful job."

Nodding, he sipped and got very creative with the ice. He took one cube between his teeth and sucked it while he smiled back at her. The rest he poured out in his hand, letting them melt through his fingers as he rubbed them on his chest. "Hot out there," he said.

"I thought it rather cool, actually."

"I noticed. You're wearing your long skirts again."

"I don't like to wear my new clothes when I'm cleaning. There's no use in—"

"Throwing good after bad," he finished for her. "So you've told me before. But have you ever stopped to think how I would feel about it?"

"I can assure you, I always wear the proper undergarments now."

"That's not what I meant." He raised the glass high, up-ending it a good ten inches above his head so the bit of liquid that was left rained on his hair. It was a rather obvious gesture, but with Sarah, he decided to pull out all the stops. He shook himself like a wet dog. She stepped back.

"What did you mean?" she asked.

"That you're ungrateful. I spent a lot of money on those clothes. I think I'm entitled to see you in them."

"As I recall, I did not want you to spend so much. You were the one who insisted."

"So I did. Did you ever think why, Sarah?"

"You told me you would feel like a better employer if I was well-clothed. I am grateful for your generosity."

"Don't think I was being generous, Sarah. I was telling the truth, but it certainly wasn't the whole truth. I wanted you even then."

"Wanted me?"

"Ever since I first saw you, I've wanted you." He noticed the pulse beating at the base of her throat and toasted her with the empty glass, adding, "In the biblical sense. Do you need a more graphic description?"

She folded her arms. "You speak of fornication."

"Is that what you call it?" Shaking his head, he set down the glass on the door of an empty stall. "Such an ugly word, Sarah. Making love is much more descriptive."

"Yet hardly accurate. There is no love between us."

He ambled over and touched her face, brushing some wisps of hair back from her forehead. "Speak for yourself."

"What are you saying?"

"It's a word, Sarah. People throw it around so much it's lost its meaning. For me, anyway. You want to use it, go right ahead."

She simply stared at him, dumbstruck.

"See what happens when you say it out loud? Traps you every time."

"You are speaking of something sacred, something holy. Love is patient and kind. It does not envy or boast. It casts out pride, selfishness and anger. It keeps no record of wrongs. Love does not delight in evil but rejoices with the truth. It always trusts, always hopes, always perseveres. It never fails."

"Maybe for you it doesn't. I prefer the more physical variety." He caught her hand, kissed her palm.

"No," she said, wrenching her arm away. "This is wrong."

"Then why does it feel so right?" he asked. "Like..." He paused dramatically. "Heaven."

"Heaven is the Kingdom of God."

"Exactly."

"You exalt me, sir. I am not your savior."

"How do you know? Maybe God sent you here on purpose."

"I believe He did. But hardly for the purpose you seem to think."

"Why not?"

"Because fornication out of wedlock is against God's law. Are you so depraved that you know nothing of His word?"

"Maybe I am. Maybe that's why God sent you here. Educate me, Sarah. Evangelize me."

His smile was very wicked now. She retreated, out of reach. "No."

"Doesn't it say somewhere in the Bible that you're supposed to be winning converts left and right? Win me, Sarah."

"You must have taken leave of your senses."

"I'm obsessed, yes. I'll concede that. Obsessed with you. Isn't that what temptation is? Aren't you here to tempt me?"

"I rather think it's the other way around."

"*I* tempt *you?* Why, Sarah, what a revelation. I had no idea."

Realizing her tactical mistake, Sarah retreated in denial. But he would have none of that. He took her hands, the softening around his mouth indulgent.

"How do I tempt you?" he asked, his tone smooth like strained honey.

"This conversation, for one," she said, summoning her most sanctimonious tone. "It is unseemly for a man and woman to speak so frankly."

He cocked his head. "Unseemly, huh? I certainly wouldn't want to be accused of that. Maybe we should let our bodies do the talking for us."

The devils were back in his eyes, beckoning her. Cheeks burning, she looked down at their joined hands. His were brown, large, and the warmth of them laced her palms. "Please, Zach. Don't say such things. I am just as human as you are."

"Are you, Sarah?" He squeezed her fingers in a gesture of sympathy.

"Yes," she whispered, daring to look at him. He was smiling a smile both tender and hungry.

"Good," he said. "That means I have a chance." His breath whispered against her lips.

She turned her face away. "No, Zach. You must understand. I am chaste and wish to remain so."

"Are you trying to tell me you're a virgin?" He chuckled and stroked her cheek with a finger. "Believe me, I figured that out a while ago."

"Then you understand why what you ask is impossible."

Both of his hands came up to cradle her face. "Sarah, all I understand is that you're drawing a line you don't want me to cross. Don't you know what a challenge that is for someone like me? I've been crossing those lines for as long as I can remember. Don't you know what a temptation you are?"

He nuzzled her lips, his mouth very warm on her skin. *No*, she thought, and closed her eyes. *But I know what a temptation you are.*

Sarah called for her will, but instead of strength she felt a drugging weakness. Like Satan himself, Zach was very skilled. He seduced with subtlety. He held her lightly, rubbing her jaw with his thumbs. He didn't push the kiss or encourage her to part her mouth. He simply caressed, touching in soft ways. There was no corner to pen her, no wall to prevent her escape. She could break away instantly.

Then why didn't she?

He lifted his head and smiled at her, but she did not smile back. She couldn't. Not when she stood shock-still, allowing him to do what he wanted. She bit her lip and searched his face, looking for answers.

Yes, he was handsome. Any woman would think so. This was a darkly appealing face equal to the ones she'd seen on billboards, advertising products. A face that spoke of rugged living, of challenges met and overcome. His body was equally eloquent. But it wasn't merely his physical looks that attracted her. It was the devils in his eyes, devils both mischievous and haunting. He had such spirit, even depraved and restless as he was. It beckoned her. In him she sensed such promise.

"Please?" he asked.

Seeing his grin made her feel light inside. He inspired a certain confidence, inducing in her a powerful wish to buy what he was selling. She *wanted* him to kiss her, stroke her, hold her. But deep in her heart she also knew he wanted only her body. Yet she couldn't give that without risking her soul.

"Why me?" she asked.

"You know what?" He kissed her forehead, speaking against it. "I've asked myself the same question. You're exactly the type of woman I usually avoid. The kind who's going to make some guy, some day, really happy."

"You compliment me, Zach. Thank you. I was afraid you didn't understand. I want to save myself for marriage."

"That's hardly fair, Sarah." She felt him brush his lips against the hair at her temple. "What if you were to die tomorrow? Wouldn't you want to have made love just once to have had the experience?"

"Only God knows when the hour of death shall come. There is little use in anticipating it."

"Sure there is. You ever wonder why death was invented? I'm convinced it's because people need to have some incentive to live life to the fullest. Let me show you how." Boldly, he touched her breast.

"No," she said, and caught his hand, stopping him. "My virginity is a gift I can give only once. I will give it to the man I marry. I will not have it taken away. I would die first."

"How dramatic, Sarah. But what if you don't marry? What if you die an old maid?"

"Then I shall be a virtuous old maid. Please, Zach."

He responded to her strong push by guiding her hands to his hips. "Just a kiss, Sarah. What harm could come from a kiss?"

Plenty, she thought, and retreated, taking her hands with her. But not before the warmth of his jeans was indelibly imprinted on the sensitive skin of her palms. She made two fists and shoved them into the pockets of her skirt. And still he pursued her, reaching out to stroke the tip of her nose with his little finger. "A kiss here, Sarah. What harm, really?"

He quickly leaned in and touched his nose to hers, then pulled away before she could protest. She was reminded of a sighting she'd once had of two wolves, the touching of noses, the way one ran, while one pursued in a simulated hunt. A mating ritual.

She shook her head emphatically. "I'd best get back to work."

"Fine by me," he said, but didn't move, blocking her path to the door. When she stepped around him, he darted in front of her again, and continued the game with every step she took, making her skin tingle with each teasing brush of his body. She wanted to laugh but didn't dare encourage him. When she finally made it to the door, he reached over her shoulder and braced his hand against the door so she couldn't open it. "What's the secret password, Sarah?"

The husky timbre of his voice weakened her knees. She knew he was right behind her, close enough to touch if she only dared. "I don't know," she said, aware of the ambivalence in her own voice.

"Guess."

"I can't." *I can't think,* she wanted to say. *Not when you're clever and endearing and oh, so bullheaded.*

"Let me give you a hint."

Suddenly his lips were under her coiled hair at the back of her neck. She shoved aside the hand holding the door, but she was clumsy and she couldn't remember if she needed to push or pull to get out. In that moment of hesitation, his hands slid around her waist. His tongue was on her now, teasing like a flicker of moist flame. She had never felt anything quite like it. It made her feel giddy inside, something he may have sensed, for his hands came up to cup her breasts, making the giddiness soar into a pleasure so intense she caught her breath.

He turned her expertly, taking advantage of her surprise, and took her mouth with his own. Only this wasn't a kiss. This was an open exploration of tongue and teeth and the fit of a male mouth against a female one. She felt it down to her toes. She grabbed his arms, his shoulders, the shaggy hair at the nape of his neck, seeking an anchor in this sudden storm. The danger was exhilarating, and she wanted more, invited more, in soundless communication. Her feet rose on tiptoe. Her body swayed, rocked against his. He answered by pushing her against the wall next to the door.

A minute ago she would have been alarmed by the violence of his reaction, but what she felt now was just as violent. It tore through her with the suddenness of a flash flood. She wanted him close. Needed him close.

He had gotten her blouse out of the waistband of her skirt without her feeling it, but his hands she did feel, hot and searching against her skin. He touched everywhere but her breasts, making her ache for the way he'd cupped them before, kneading them with his long fingers. She arched her back, pressing against his chest, but it wasn't enough. The motion of her mouth echoed the push of her hips against his.

Oh, Lord. She wanted him so badly.

She tore her mouth away from his and stared. He did, too, looking as aroused as she felt. His blue eyes were keen with it, and called to her with a hunger she couldn't ignore. She had thought the tugging of her heart hard to resist. But this was worse, shaking her to her bones. A terrible, wonderful temptation. She suddenly understood the lesson in a verse from the Song of Solomon.

I am my beloved's, and his desire is toward me.

She hadn't understood the link between her body and her soul until this moment. Desire was a living thing, building naturally until it burst, bright and strong. The Apostle Paul had been correct. Love wasn't wrong. Nor was it something to be feared. Love fed her spirit, reaching upward, outward, seeking the light in the eyes of her beloved. Zach's eyes.

They were a kaleidoscope in turquoise and gray, searching hers. Always searching. She felt the hardness of his body through the layers of clothing between them. So little separated them. And so much.

"No," she whispered.

"Yes." He lowered his head and kissed her softly. The pressure of tears built behind her eyes. She shook her head and his mouth moved with hers, expertly persuasive. Her hands tangled in his hair, disobedient, but her heart was more wise, and a tear slipped from under her lashes. She cared about this man. And it tore at her, what she was contemplating, because she did care about him, very much.

"Zach, please, you must listen to me."

"I'm listening," he said into her mouth.

"No, you're not." She shoved, her hands clenched in distress, and when he would have caught them, she raised one and slapped his face.

"No!"

He rubbed the mark reddening his jaw, his gaze oddly triumphant, as turbulent as a stormy sky.

"Don't ever do this to me again," she cried, and fled.

Nobility, Zach discovered, was a difficult master. It didn't help that he had so little practice at behaving with someone else's best interests in mind. He tried treating Sarah like a queen. The Snow Queen. He saw her every day for a week and never touched her. At least, not on purpose.

The hundred little accidents—the brush of her sleeve when he reached for his coffee, the press of his palm on her shoulder when he sat down next to her at the supper table, the flick of a finger when he passed platters of food to her—didn't count. Neither did the searing looks he sent her way, the ones that made her blush. They didn't count because they caused him more pain than they did her. Awful pain. Terrible pain. The pain of knowing he could never have her. And as long as he was subjecting himself to the greater torture, he could get away with calling himself noble.

She, on the other hand, was anything but. Sarah wore her heart on her sleeve. Her eyes followed him when they were in the same room, and more than once she brought lemonade to him when he was alone finishing up repairs to the barn. Curiously, these were the times he relaxed his guard, for she practiced none of the arts of a seductress. Instead she talked, telling him bits about her day. He found himself listening to her in a way he hadn't ever done before. As though he really cared.

The thing that saved him was Brazil. He'd promised Manuelo he'd return by the end of October, just two weeks away. Zach refused to go back on his word this time. Already, thanks to his work and that of the ranch hands, the cattle were all sold, the crops harvested and the buildings in good enough shape to command top dollar. And so he put the wheels in motion for the sale.

The real-estate agent was very optimistic. The town of Boulder was growing at great pace, and large tracts of land were hard to come by. Builders were scrambling for anything they could subdivide and erect single-family houses on. Zach put out of his mind what that might mean for Sarah, the hands, or the Bar M itself. Years ago, he'd told himself it didn't matter what happened to the ranch. Now it was time to prove it.

The day came right on schedule, five days before Halloween. An early winter snow drove him into the tiny bunkhouse office to put the finishing touches on the ranch books. When the real-estate agent called, it didn't take a genius to recognize the offer was generous, designed to get him to accept on the spot. He would have, too, but lately he'd grown less impulsive, less willing to go hell-bent for leather at the slightest provocation.

"I'll get back to you tomorrow," Zach said.

He left the bunkhouse and headed to the barn, then thought better of riding Nutkin, though the mare needed a good run. He wanted to think, not distract himself.

He veered west and put his head down against the stiff wind blowing from the northwest. He tucked his hands more firmly into the heavy coat he'd borrowed from Coburn and kept his eyes on the ground. Fifty minutes later he arrived at the bank of the creek where he had first seen Sarah, four weeks ago.

Seeing the place made the decision easy. Of course he would sell. Of course he would tell her goodbye. These were the absolutes of his life. He wanted no ties to the past, and certainly nothing that tied him to the future. He would return to Brazil having dispensed with everything that had ever held him back in his life.

He looked at the ridge, at the faint outline of mountains beyond. He would never come back. And though he knew he was doing the right thing, it hurt inside, in a way he couldn't explain. Even though the ranch symbolized all he had rejected in his life, he would miss it. The land, the mountains, the crisp clear air. God, how he would miss it.

And her.

Taking care to keep well-hidden, Sarah knelt on the rocky ground on top of the ridge and peered down. Zach stood on the creek back below, staring at the icy water, a motionless figure among the stark, leafless trees. A chill ran through her, caused not as much by the wintry wind as the lonely look of him. She recognized a farewell scene when she saw one.

In the past week since the kiss in the barn, she'd thought much about why she felt so drawn to him. But it wasn't until today, now, that she understood. For she could see that it was as difficult for him as it had been for her to say goodbye to the only home he had ever known.

She wanted to go down there and tell him that he didn't have to grieve—that in whatever new place he made his home, he would find the solace he was searching for. Yet she knew it wasn't true. Maybe it was true for her—but not Zach. Because he couldn't make a new home without facing what had destroyed the old one.

The house, she thought. It always came back to the house—and the family which once had lived there.

She could see it clearly, what the rejection of his roots had done to him, both good and bad. Yes, it taught him self-reliance, how to be capable and strong, to be able to meet any challenge, anywhere. But it also kept him isolated and aloof, unwilling to appreciate the gifts given to him. Especially those that had to do with the Bar M.

So a great horseman and cattleman was lost to the wilds of Brazil. Perhaps that wasn't such a tragedy—the wilderness was the only food available to a lost soul. But it left him without roots, without peace. And she couldn't bear to watch someone she cared about live without peace. She needed to reach out to him in a way he wouldn't reject, and soon. The ranch was ready to be put on the market and she was running out of time.

The kiss in the barn had made her realize something else about herself. How human she was, and how vulnerable. In the Bible, temptation sounded like such a cut-and-dried thing, a simple question of right and wrong. It was wrong of him to pressure her so, to make light of her beliefs. But what was right about standing by and watching a man get ready to sell what was essentially his soul—the very place of his birth?

Very slowly, Sarah withdrew from her perch on the rocky ridge. She took the long route back to the house, ambling aimlessly, thinking, praying. What would it take to get him to see the light?

The answer came to her when she stepped into the yard and Butcher came running to greet her. Not wanting to tip off Zach that she was following him, she'd bade Butcher to stay behind. Now the dog was so glad to see her he ran around in circles, yowling joyfully.

It was the joy that got to her, the sight of such love and devotion. This is what Zach lacked.

Kneeling in the dirt, she hugged the wriggling dog. He snuffled loudly and licked her chin. Laughing, she held him off by pushing him back and rubbing his ears. "That's my boy," she murmured. "I love you, too."

Butcher lay down, rolled over and stretched out his head, exposing his neck for a good, long scratch. The ultimate show of trust moved her beyond words, for he was completely at her mercy, exposing the lifeblood just beneath his throat.

Her hands gentled as she looked at him, and an idea took hold, one that seized her with instant clarity. Of course. She would offer the same type of trust to Zach. Why hadn't she thought of it before?

A quiver of fear ran through her. Because he'd take full advantage of it, that's why. In order to make this work, she had to offer herself in concrete terms, body and soul. She had to do more than admit she loved him. She had to be willing to show him, too.

Lord, what was she contemplating?

The scene in the barn came back to her in full force along with the dreadful teetering of her conscience. Could she really trust him not to take what he had said he most wanted—her?

Sarah gazed at Butcher, stretched out in ecstasy. Or did the real question involve something else? Could she really trust herself not to take what she most wanted—him?

Eight

Two days later Zach told Sarah to prepare a special noon meal for the ranch hands. At the end of it, he announced that he'd accepted an offer and that the ranch had been officially sold the previous day. Under the terms of the contract, he had one month to vacate the place. Though they were welcome to leave anytime, he promised they'd be paid through the next four weeks, and said point-blank he couldn't guarantee any jobs with the new owner because a developer had bought the property and planned to turn it into a residential community.

A long silence filled the bunkhouse kitchen. Miller was the first to break it. He shoved his dessert plate forward, stood, jammed his hat on his head, and stomped out.

"Sorry, Sarah. I ain't too hungry anymore, either." Coburn also rose and the other two ranch hands followed, leaving Zach and Sarah alone.

"I'll clean up," Zach offered peremptorily, "if you want to march out of here, too."

"When are you leaving?"

Her question was softly spoken, without a trace of rancor. Maybe he should have expected that, knowing Sarah, but he found himself even more impressed because he understood how hard this must be for her. "The day after tomorrow, when I'm sure all the official papers are signed. Coburn and the real-estate agent will take care of the rest."

She nodded and took a small bite of her meal, her expression thoughtful.

"What will you do?" he asked.

"Before coming here, I'd planned to winter in Boulder. I expect I might still do that. Find a job, a place to live..."

Zach picked up his coffee mug and sipped. "What about your stepfather?"

"What about him?"

"Are you worried that he's out there, looking for you?"

"I don't know," she said, and leaned back in her chair. "Perhaps it is foolish to worry. I do know I want to feel safe wherever I may end up."

"Would you consider coming to work for me in Brazil?" The question just popped out, yet when he heard it, he felt how much he wanted her to say yes.

"Brazil?" she echoed. Her gaze narrowed as she studied him. "Doing what?"

"Just what you've been doing here. Cooking, cleaning, creating a—" *Home*, he almost said. "A place where people feel welcome. Even scientists on an Amazon adventure like their comfort, and Manuelo and I do have the odd tourist group once in a while. Our clients expect a good meal and a clean bed to sleep in."

"And what would you expect, Zach?"

"I'm not going to lie to you, Sarah. I would expect you to live with me."

"I thought you might say that." The sadness in her smile spoke volumes.

Zach realized he was going to have to come up with something a lot better than a live-in maid. He put down the mug and took up one of her hands, sandwiching it between both of his. "In return, I'm willing to marry you at the end of next year, if we both think it's the right thing to do."

Her eyes widened.

"I know, I know. I told you I'd never get married. But I find myself willing to make an exception—in your case."

He said it with a lopsided grin, meaning it as a compliment, but she looked at him with something akin to disappointment in her eyes. "A year's time?"

"I need to be sure this is the best thing for both of us."

"And living in sin is the right thing?"

"Sarah, listen to me. I know this goes against everything you've been taught. But try to see it from my point of view. My parents thought they belonged together and look what happened to them. Their long and bitter divorce completely split my family. Bram, my older brother, is on his second marriage—his first was a disaster. Can you blame me for wanting to be careful about how I go about this?"

"No, I cannot blame you. But neither can I change the person that I am."

"You should know that I've never asked a woman to live with me before. My personal freedom means too much to me. But I'm asking you, Sarah."

"Why?"

The $64,000 question. "Why do you think?"

"Because you've come to care for me?"

"Something like that."

"I see."

"I think it may be a stronger feeling than that," he amended, unable to say the L word. It was too binding, and he needed to be absolutely, positively sure of his feelings before he made such a commitment. Hers, too. Yet he could feel how much she expected it. He got down on one knee, hoping to show what he couldn't say. "Will you come to Brazil with me, Sarah?"

"We would live in the jungle?"

"My base camp is located in a simple village on the river, where the people live much like they do in the Community you've told me so much about. I think you'll appreciate it as few can."

"Are there mountains in this place?"

"No," he said, squeezing her hand. "Not like here. But it's green and full of life. You can have a garden like you've never dreamed of."

"What if I don't like it, Zach? I've never lived anywhere but here and Montana, and they are very much the same, with the vast landscape and open sky."

"There are places like that all over the world. I'd love to show you."

"What about staying here?"

His grip tightened. "That's not possible, Sarah. The Bar M is gone now."

"Yes," she said. "I can see that it is."

He waited, unwilling to say anything that might betray his chances. He'd known this would be hard, humbling himself in this way, and he chafed again at the power she had over him. But it would be worth it if she agreed to go with him.

"Before I give you my answer about Brazil, I have a request to make, one I've been mulling over for some time."

A feeling of dread washed over him because he knew what she was going to say. "Sarah, the ranch is sold, along with the house. Having me look around inside is not going to change anything."

"I want you to tell me I did a good job."

"I don't need to look to tell you that, Sarah. You tackle everything with painstaking thoroughness. I'm sure you did a terrific job."

"I want you to see for yourself. I won't believe the house is presentable otherwise."

"The new owner will serve as my eyes and ears. He'll let me know if anything needs to be changed."

"I am willing to strike a bargain with you in order to convince you."

"Really?" Sarah's brand of bargaining usually had interesting results. "What kind of bargain?"

"My body. I will lie with you as David did with Bathsheba."

Zach almost fell over. "You can't be serious."

"It is something you want, is it not?"

"What about all that stuff you told me about saving yourself for marriage?"

"You spoke of how much your freedom means to you. This means much to me, as well."

"Sarah, it's just a house."

"It is more than a house. It is a home. Once you see the inside, I'm sure you will think of it differently."

"You'll think I'll experience some kind of epiphany if I go inside? It's not going to happen, Sarah. I don't care what you've done to it, that house is still the place where I grew up. And I'll never be able to forget the things that happened there."

Sarah pressed her lips together in an inward search to explain herself. How do you offer hope to a man who has long ago given it up? "You would reject me, then?" she asked, meeting his gaze directly.

His eyes narrowed and she knew he had correctly interpreted the challenge in her voice. "Don't play games with me, Sarah. If you are serious about this, there's no going back."

"I have never been more serious about anything in my life," she insisted.

He hesitated, his thumb tight on the rapid pulse of her wrist. "You want me to inspect the house. That's all?" he asked.

"Yes."

"How long will it take?"

"Long enough to see every room."

"Which comes first, my part of the bargain or yours?"

"Yours," she said quickly.

"Not a chance," Zach said, needing to test just how far she was willing to go. "Either we sleep together first, or there's no deal."

"Sleep together?"

"A figure of speech," he explained. "Which in this case fits. I want you beside me the entire night."

Nerves jumped along her limbs. "All night?"

"If this is to be our first chance to be together, I want you there when I fall asleep and I want you there in the morning when I wake up."

Sarah swallowed, but she had gone too far to back down now. He was leaving in two days. Time had run out. And she had a certain faith the Lord was leading her down this path. Somehow, some way, He would make everything all right. "Where would we do this thing?"

Zach returned to his chair, using the movement as a chance to think. The trailer would be the logical place, but he couldn't bring himself to suggest it. They'd be cramped in the small bed, and there was something profane about taking Sarah in a tin can of a room a stone's throw from the bunkhouse where the ranch hands would be.

"We'll go to a hotel," he said.

"Like *Pretty Woman*—that movie with the prostitute?"

Suddenly Zach didn't want to go to a hotel. "Do you have a better suggestion?"

"The house. It seems only fair. Then one of us cannot back out on the other."

He shook his head. Yet inwardly he couldn't help but acknowledge that the house answered his most important criteria—privacy. And she had a point about the terms. They would be meeting them simultaneously. "What about Butcher?" he asked. "The house is his territory. He won't like having me there."

"I will see to it that he doesn't bother you—us."

Seeing the color leaping on her face, Zach knew he shouldn't go along with this harebrained scheme. She would regret it, and probably so would he.

He looked down at their joined hands and thought back to the time he had first seen her, outlined against rushing whitewater and an afternoon sun, blinding in her grace. He'd vowed then to have her. And here she was, offering to sleep with him. Willingly, without any guarantees for the future. If she said no to Brazil, he would at least have a chance of getting over his obsession with her. The price might be high, but the reward was higher, higher than he'd ever imagined. He'd still be free.

"You drive a hard bargain, Sarah Smith."

She shook his proffered hand and rose, agreeing to meet at the house after supper. After she left, Zach went to the window to watch her cross the yard, her posture as regal as ever. He should feel triumphant. Except he didn't. He felt sad somehow. But the sadness didn't make him change his mind.

He was going to make love to her.

His anticipation increased the closer the clock ticked to suppertime. At five, he quit early to shower and shave, though he put on a clean T-shirt and pair of jeans for the evening so as not to alert the men that anything out of the ordinary was in store for the night. Sarah, too, wore her usual working clothes while she dished out supper. She ate very little and he could tell she was nervous. Nervous as a new bride.

Feeling curiously tender, he offered to clean up the dishes, and she accepted, murmuring her thanks. But it was her secret squeeze of his hand, hidden from the other men, which made her gratitude hit home. He reflected on the feeling after she left, and for the first time it occurred to him that maybe, just maybe, she wanted to be with him as much as he wanted to be with her.

He must be far gone.

When the dishes were put away, he said good-night to the men and headed for the house by way of the barn, in case anyone was watching. As he strode along, he realized he should have brought something. Champagne, flowers, candy, *something*.

He checked the darkening sky, figured he had a few extra minutes and turned around. When he walked up the flagstone path ten minutes later he had a bottle of wine in one hand and a bouquet of late-blooming pansies in the other.

He didn't feel any real anxiety until he reached the bottom of the porch steps. He paused, overtaken by the deep feeling of claustrophobia the house always engendered in him. The roof loomed over him like the lid of a coffin.

The front door opened, spilling light across the porch. He looked up and gripped the porch railing.

Sarah was wearing blue jeans. *Blue jeans.* Like a second skin, the denim hugged her slim legs, making them appear even longer. Her silk blouse was one he'd bought her during that first shopping trip at the mall. The creamy color matched her skin. Her hair was up, and there was something different about the style. She had twisted it higher on her head and left a few soft tendrils falling around her face.

Good Lord.

"Come in," she said. "It's cold out there."

He climbed one porch stair, then another, until he reached the threshold of the door. Escaping heat from the house washed over him. She stepped back, gesturing him in, but he didn't move.

Her hand reached out and grabbed his sleeve. She reeled him inside, but the shutting of the door sounded so final he had an urge to grab her right then, like a drowning man. Instead he concentrated on the details of her appearance, noting the careful way she had prepared herself, just for him. She'd applied just a touch of lip gloss, giving her mouth the hue of crushed strawberries. Her eyes were huge, the irises nearly black, while her cheeks were pale. Still nervous, he thought.

"I brought you these," he said, thrusting the bouquet of pansies into her hands.

"How pretty." She buried her nose in the jumble of delicate flowers and her eyelashes came down, hiding her thoughts. "No one's ever given me flowers before."

"It's a tradition."

"A tradition?"

"To bring flowers."

"A nice tradition," she said. "Thank you."

"I brought wine, too. A California Chardonnay. Nineteen-eighty-nine was a good year."

She nodded but the description obviously meant nothing to her and Zach regretted his words. *A good year?* He was more nervous than she was.

"May I take your coat?" she asked.

He hesitated, loathe to give up the armor it represented. But the heated interior of the house was very warm.

"Thanks," he said, and shrugged it off. She set the flowers and wine down on a nearby table and hung his coat on a bentwood hall tree set in the corner by the front door.

The stretch of her body, so clearly defined in tight denim and clingy silk, made Zach breathe deep. Scents assaulted his nose. Cinnamon, fresh paint, and lemon wax. He recalled his promise, won at such great personal cost to her. He'd agreed to this tour. He might be a scoundrel to make her go through with her part of it, but he would be an honorable one.

"Mind if I look around?"

She glanced at him and he saw a slight hint of color come back into her cheeks. "Please do."

Resolutely he headed down the hall. He didn't remember the row of gleaming brass wall sconces that ran the length of the wall. To his left was the staircase that led to the second floor. To the right was the arched opening of the front room, the setting for many a family fight.

He poked his head inside, intent on making the most cursory of examinations. What hit him first were the windows. She'd removed all the heavy avocado-green draperies that had once hung over them, ceiling-to-floor. Now they were framed by panels of white lace, parted to reveal the clarity of the glass. Each pane sparkled, backed by a velvet night. Sunny yellow walls enriched the feeling of contrast. The dull braided rug he remembered from his childhood was gone, revealing an oak plank floor polished to honeyed perfection. He stepped forward, amazed at the transformation. Yet everything he saw, he recognized.

His mother's antique rocker stood in one corner, lamplight glossing the scrolled armrests. The spindle-backed bench set along the opposite wall looked uncomfortable as hell but its finish matched the chair, lending unity. Needlepoint pillows were propped in the corners.

Last but not least was the fireplace. The scratched mahogany mantel had been painted white. Set on top were dozens of candles in different colors and sizes, all set in brass holders.

"Where did you find these?" he asked, and went to pick up a candlestick, his memory stirring.

"The attic." She hung back in the hall, watching him. "Do you remember seeing them before?"

"Whenever us kids had a birthday, my mom would get these out so everyone would have a chance to make a wish and blow out the candles."

"Make a wish and blow out the candles? Whatever for?"

"Tradition. When a birthday is celebrated, a cake is made and little candles are placed on top, one for each year of age. Before you blow them out, you make a wish, and if you can get them all in one breath, your wish will come true."

"What kind of wish?"

"Anything you want," he said, noting how she lingered at the doorway. "The bigger and more impossible, the better."

"Really?" She sketched a slippered toe on the burnished floor, the curve of her mouth wistful. "And it always comes true?"

"If you wish for it hard enough and don't peek, then yes, it always comes true."

"What did you wish on your last birthday?"

"Sorry, I can't tell. That's one of the rules. If you confess your wish, it doesn't have a chance." He set the candlestick down and picked up a box of matches. "Would you like to try?"

"It's not my birthday."

"Let's pretend it is." He lit a candle. "Come here."

Sarah hesitated, but he held the candle out to her, his manner as whimsical and endearing as ever. He gave her no choice other than to make a fuss or obey. She chose the latter and stopped in front of him. "What do I do?" she asked.

He reached past her to flick the light switch. The lamps in the room went off, leaving only the light coming in from the hall. The flame from the candle sent shadows leaping across his face, heightening the demon wings of his dark eyebrows. "Like I said. Make a wish and blow it out."

Hesitant, she waited a moment, then dutifully pursed her lips and blew. The space between them plunged into relative darkness. All she could see clearly was the flash of his teeth, framed by a ghostly grin.

"Now kiss me," he said.

"Is that part of the tradition, too?"

She glowed with barely discernible color, her purity obvious in the clean lines of her face. Yet her eyes reflected the night, a night Zach wanted to lose himself in. "Yes," he lied.

He had to go very still to feel the soft press of lips against his own. Unused to the role of aggressor, her mouth was tentative, a scant weight against his. Yet what she offered was so sweet. Like the trust of a tiny bird come to feed from a human hand. How courageous she was, he thought. And he had to fight a tough battle within himself not to take advantage of that.

He let her drop back and come down off her toes without touching her in any way, then flipped the light switch back on.

"Did I displease you?" she asked, clearly confused.

"No," he said, giving her his most sincere smile. "I just wanted to prove to you that I'm not going to attack you at the first opportunity. We have all night, right?"

She blinked and nodded.

He took her hand, noting how clammy it still was. "What else did you want to show me?"

She led him back down the hallway toward the rear of the house. A hallway filled not only with light, but life. Life in pictures.

It was the first thing his father had done after the divorce—to remove every reminder of Mary Masterson's presence. Zach could barely remember decorations ever being on the walls, much less family pictures.

The photographs Sarah had unearthed were of happier times. Times, Zach, in all honesty, could not remember. He'd been too much of a baby. If he was in a picture at all, it showed him barely out of diapers. As the youngest in the family, he was invariably in the forefront, framed by an even collection of brothers and sisters, boy-girl, boy-girl. Bram, Liz, Joe, Meg and he.

"Do you mind that I put these up?" Sarah asked, slipping an arm through his. "I knew it would be only temporary, but the house does have a history. I wanted to show it."

"No, I don't mind," Zach said, and proved the claim by examining each photo in detail, marveling at how detached he felt. Even the wedding portrait of his parents didn't move him. They appeared like any couple who thought themselves in love. Rather young and foolish-looking.

She showed him the room tucked at the end of the hall, a den Zach remembered as dark-paneled and gloomy, crammed with books and files and a massive rolltop desk. Now it was filled with colors—pumpkin orange, deep russet and forest green. And mostly, the glossy chestnut brown of thoroughly polished antique mahogany.

Every book remaining on the wall-to-ceiling shelves had been cleaned. All hardcovers, they glowed with the patina of aged leather. In the spaces between the shortened stacks, she'd taken dozens of clay pots and planted what he recognized as common herbs. Parsley and basil trailed fresh green shoots from the lush soil of their new homes.

His father's old desk sat in the middle of the room, rolled open. Each cubbyhole had been meticulously cleaned out. Nothing lay on the polished surface except an old leather-bound ledger.

Zach kept waiting for some memory to hit him like a two-by-four, but the impact was more subtle than that. He could remember Dad spending many an evening at this desk, slaving over the ranch books, his back bent in subjugation.

With the decline of the cattle industry in the seventies, Matthew Masterson had done everything he could to make the Bar M into a successful farming operation. He'd expanded, buying more land to the east. What he hadn't counted on was the rise and fall of inflation. Once property values crashed, loans were called, and he'd lost everything he'd bought, plus half of the original ranch he'd put up as collateral. From that point on, the family had lived on the edge of subsistence, always waiting for that year that would make or break them.

A feeling of failure permeated the atmosphere of the house in those days. Zach had hated it and so had his mother. She had not been able to stand the uncertainty of living hand to mouth. Neither could his father, for that matter. But that was something Matthew Masterson had never been able to admit.

Sarah tugged his arm, making Zach realize how long he'd been staring at the desk. "What do you think?" she asked.

Wanting to shield her from his gloomy thoughts, he tucked a wisp of hair behind her ear. "I think you've been working too hard."

It must not have been the right thing to say for she withdrew and headed down the hall toward the kitchen. He followed the pinwheel of brown formed by the hair loosely coiled at the back of her head. Gold, sienna and red threaded rich coffee black.

"Sarah, I'm sorry," he said as he entered the kitchen. "The den looked great. It really did."

He halted, the heels of his boots sounding loud to his ears. This had been his mother's domain and he didn't even recognize it. Open, airy, the room reflected Sarah's personality now. The once-stained cabinets had been painted white, matching a bow-fronted refrigerator, dishwasher and oven. Every surface gleamed.

"Wow," he said.

She placed her hand at her brow in a mock swoon, and he felt her pleasure at his unguarded reaction. This was how he would always remember her, standing in a kitchen with a smile of delight on her face. This room defined her best, the heart and soul of any house, the gathering place for those who needed sustenance.

Nine

Sarah sat Zach down at the kitchen table and plied him with a piece of apple pie and a cup of coffee. She was rapidly running out of things to show him. Only the upstairs remained with its five bedrooms. Lord knew she wasn't quite ready to face the big one with the four-poster.

Luckily Zach didn't appear to mind. He sprawled in the ladder-back kitchen chair, lazily eating his pie, surprising her with his ease. She hadn't expected that. He wasn't reacting to her or the house in the way she'd forecast at all.

He was telling her stories, funny ones about his growing up years, even those succeeding his parents' divorce. Apparently, he'd been quite the rebel, and judging by the fondness of the recollections, proud of it, as well.

Zach admitted his father hadn't felt the same, of course. What father would? Yet Sarah didn't hear the pain of a son misunderstood. Instead Zach appeared to be saying just the opposite—that he, not his father, was the one to blame.

Sarah leaned across the kitchen table, her eyes seeking his. "It's not your fault," she said out of the blue, taking a stab in the dark.

"Sure it is. I could never be what my father wanted me to be. I didn't even try."

"What did he want you to be?"

Zach laid down his fork. "He needed me to help with chores, to toe the line, and become exactly the same thing he was. And you can bet I always did the opposite of what he said."

"You were a child then, were you not?"

"Farm kids have to grow up fast, Sarah. You know that. And you can take my word for it—children of divorce grow up even faster."

She reached across to touch his hand, but he got up to carry his dishes from the table.

"Everyone he ever loved turned against him. He never got over my mom leaving him or the splitting of the family. How could he? I, for one, wouldn't let him forget it. I screwed up in school, in church, in 4-H, any place I could. Even when he died, I came back, not for the funeral but to shut up this house. It was my way of thumbing my nose at his memory. And that's when I began my campaign to talk the rest of my family into selling everything he'd spent his life saving."

"Which you have done."

"Yes." The dishes clinked in the sink and he turned to face her, arms crossed over his chest. "How will you be able to leave this place, after putting in so much of yourself?"

"I shall weep," she admitted. "But this is to be the home of another. I only hope the family that buys it will be happy here."

Zach didn't have the heart to tell her the developer would either move all the ranch buildings to another location, or tear them down. Either prospect was depressing, even to him, so he pushed it from his mind the same way he pushed everything from his mind. He rebelled. "You remind me of my father, Sarah. Have you noticed? I always want to be the opposite of what you want, as well.''

Sarah knew he was being facetious, for the devils had come back to his eyes and he was suddenly restless, though he scarcely moved. Only his hand came up in a tiny motion while a smile carved his face. He crooked his index finger at her.

Her breath filled her throat. Very slowly, she spread her hands on the table, needing to feel something solid beneath her palms. Using the table for support, she rose, and just as slowly, went to stand in front of him.

"So hesitant, Sarah. Were you hoping I would let you out of your part of the bargain?''

She couldn't bear to tell the truth and say yes, so she said nothing, unwilling to share the secrets of her soul. This part was between her and God, anyway, for it had been in her nightly Bible reading that she had justified this idea to offer her body to Zach. After all, in Genesis, Abraham had offered his only begotten son as proof of his faith. Her virginity seemed a small thing in comparison.

Zach twined a finger around one of the wispy curls that had fallen around her face. He spoke no words. There was only the hungry roaming of his eyes upon her face.

"There are many other rooms upstairs you haven't seen yet," she whispered.

"There's only one room I want to see right now," he said, pressing the promise of a soft kiss against her cheek. "The one with the biggest bed."

And so it begins, she thought.

She took his hand and led him back through the long hallway and up the stairs to his parents' old room. Zach watched her open the door and step aside, her eyes downcast. He'd guessed this was the room she slept in. Lord knew, he had imagined her enough, stretched across the wide bed, tangled in sheets and blankets and little else. But to see her here in the flesh brought it home to him, how dry

his imagination had been. Colorless, textureless, defined by
raw desire rather than Sarah's reality.

He stepped past her and flipped on the lights. The first
thing he noticed was the quilt she had hung behind the bed.
Blue was the dominant color in the wedding-ring design, a
restful powder blue that was picked up in the throw pillows, the skirted table between the windows and, especially, the walls. Even the ceiling was painted blue, making
him think of the Colorado sky. There was no bluer sky in all
the world.

The bed was covered in white chenille. A spinning wheel
stood on the far side, unearthed from the attic no doubt, for
Zach couldn't remember ever seeing it before. There actually was a skein of thick yarn wrapped around the spindle
and puffs of raw wool in a basket underneath.

"It relaxes me," Sarah said, catching him staring.

He glanced at her. She had gone completely pale,
bleached by the incandescent light.

"Don't forget to look at the bathroom," she said, moving swiftly to open another door, revealing a small space
tiled in black and white. Light blue towels hung from various brass bars. The claw-footed tub was an immaculate
white as were the matching pedestal sinks. "Nice," he said,
without taking his eyes off her face.

She bit her lip and retreated back to the bedroom. He
followed, wondering why he had ever let her talk him into
coming here. But he knew why. The answer lay in the heavy
beat of his blood. Even now, with all he'd encountered in
regard to the house and Sarah's reticence, the one feeling
that overrode all else was lust.

"Have you any candles up here?" he asked.

She went to one of the small tables set on either side of the
bed and held up two old-fashioned brass candle holders,
complete with blue tapers.

"Light them both, Sarah," he said, and removed his
boots.

"I'd prefer the dark."

"I want to see you, Sarah. All of you."

She took up a box of matches, struck once, twice, three times, before the flame burst. Her front teeth caught her lower lip as she lit the two wicks, the trembling of her fingers obvious in the shadows wavering on the wall. She blew out the flame, tucked the charred matchstick into one brass holder, then carried the second to the other side of the bed.

He switched off the lights. She put the candle down, kicked off her slippers and glanced down at herself before she abruptly turned around, standing with her back to him, the ivory nape of her neck revealed. The subtle movement of her bent elbows told him she was fumbling with the buttons of her blouse.

"Don't," he said.

She glanced askance at him, hands poised above her breasts. "Is this not how the act is done?"

"I want to undress you myself."

Her mouth opened to protest.

"But not yet," he soothed, and drew her ice-cold hands away from her blouse. He led her to the dressing table next to a tall five-drawer bureau. "I have something else in mind first."

"You do?" A crease worried her brow, making her appear very young.

He smiled. "Do you have a hairbrush?"

"What would you need a hairbrush for?"

"To brush your hair with, silly."

Her clenched fingers relaxed slightly. "You wish to brush my hair?"

"If you'll let me."

She retrieved her brush from a drawer and gave it to him. He put his hand on her shoulder and guided her to the little vanity bench, so she faced the oval mirror above the table. Her reflected face still looked very white. He positioned himself behind her and began to pluck the pins from her hair.

"Close your eyes," he said.

She hesitated. He rubbed the base of her neck, loosening the knot of tension beneath her unraveling hair and bent so she could see his face next to hers.

"Please?"

Her hands came together in her lap in a tight clench. Very slowly, her eyelashes lowered, becoming feathery crescents against her fine-grained skin. The bristles of the brush made a soft sound. It underlined the building silence in the room. Zach began to hum under his breath, suggesting the melody of "Amazing Grace," her favorite hymn. She cocked her head to listen.

Candlelight brought out the red tones in her hair, making it ignite in his hands like a river of flame. After a long while he put down the brush and combed her hair with his fingers, letting it curl over his wrists.

As always, she was oblivious to what she did to him. He pulled out a front section of her hair and guided it so a long curl fell over her shoulder. His fingers contrasted sharply with the soft cream of her blouse. Gentle heat beckoned him through the silk. Using a forefinger, he stroked the skin beneath her collar, tracing the line of her neck as it curved into her body.

Her eyes flew open. Keeping his finger inside her blouse, he dragged his hand upward and found the bones of her face. She relaxed. Her cheeks had a special warmth all their own. He cupped her blush with his palms and watched her eyes darken as they took in the erotic contrast between his tanned hands and the ivory planes of her face.

His thumbs crept up and framed her forehead, rubbing away the lines of tension. She made a small sound. He rubbed harder and circled her temples. She sighed and the point of her chin came down on a sigh.

He massaged her neck and shoulders. Gradually she went limp all over and he knelt behind the little stool and whispered, "Remember how you feel right now."

She raised her head, reflecting her hesitant nod. Her eyes were sleepy, the pupils dilated and filled with a lovely sheen. He reached around her neck and undid the top button of her blouse, watching his progress in the mirror. She sat very still, like a statue. He undid the next button and the next, working his way downward until he reached the waistband of her jeans.

He tore his gaze from her reflection and looked down over her shoulder. The cleft between her breasts was framed by the ivory lace cups of her bra. To expose her more fully, all he needed to do was pull apart her blouse.

He shrugged out of his shirt. Above the rigid line of her shoulders, his chest looked golden in the flickering candle-light. Without preamble, he snaked his hands around her waist. She inhaled sharply, reflexively drawing back. But he was right behind her and she had nowhere to go. His hands slid inside her open blouse and discovered the plane of her stomach, taut with tension. He pressed one palm flat against it.

Her breath caught. Smiling a little, he skimmed his way to her half-hidden breasts and watched for her reaction. She arched back further, trapping her head against his shoulder. Her blouse gaped open, revealing the lacy cups of her bra and the half-moons of flesh above.

He covered her breasts with his hands and filled his palms with warm lace. She was unbelievably soft and the silk sliding over the backs of his hands was the same texture. The sight of him touching her so intimately excited him no end. Staying in place behind her chair, he nuzzled the nape of her neck, relishing the rush of blood pooling in his loins. He had waited for this moment far too long.

Up close, she smelled like roses, spicy and feminine. He burrowed his nose beneath the folded edge of her collar and kissed the point where neck met shoulder, lingering over the salty taste of her skin. She tilted her head and he took full advantage, laving her bared shoulder with his tongue, wishing he could lick her everywhere at the same time.

Patience, he told himself. Patience. Still, the fantasy drove him and before he knew it, he'd flicked open the front clasp of her bra. Her bare breasts filled his hands. He cupped and lifted and felt her nipples pucker against his palm.

Delighted by her responsiveness, he examined her face in the mirror. Her eyes were closed and her mouth was slightly parted, revealing the barest hint of teeth. He rubbed his jaw against her cheek and she turned toward him, seeking his mouth.

To touch her freely while he kissed her was heaven. The angle wasn't square, so he captured her lower lip between his teeth and gently sucked. Finally he rubbed his thumb along her jawline and pressed the corner of her mouth. Using the hint of moisture he found there, he wet her lips.

She opened her eyes. Haunted by what he saw in them, Zach whispered in her ear. "I promise I'll do everything possible not to hurt you."

"I know," she whispered, though her vulnerable expression didn't change.

A rush of empathy took him out of his body and into hers. She had a right to be scared. She had never done this before. Taking her hands, he pulled her up. "Let's dance."

"Dance?"

"Haven't you heard of it?" he asked, quickly buttoning her blouse.

"Of course," Sarah said, unsure what to make of this new development. "But how can we? There is no music."

"Can't you hear it?"

Taking her hands, he hummed a quick tune and swung her around in a sudden, breathless circle. "Oh!" she cried, grabbing his arms.

"Too fast?"

She nodded and his biceps bulged as he lifted her and set her squarely in front of him, a foot away. He pressed her left hand to his shoulder and pulled her right hand sideways so their two arms, linked together, completed the classic dancer's embrace.

"We'll waltz, then, nice and slow."

"But I don't know how."

"Neither do I. We can fake it, though." Humming a heavily cadenced version of the "Blue Danube," which he recalled from the movie *2001*, Zach guided her slowly around the room, not quite sure if he should be leading with his left foot or his right. Sarah's face was a study in concentration. She tried to keep up with him, but she kept stumbling and he sensed how her courage was being sucked under by the brave front she was putting on to please him.

Zach abandoned the waltz, circled her waist and pulled her close. "When in doubt, do the box step," he said against the shell of her ear, wishing he knew the magic words that would ease her fears. He led her in a simple square but couldn't hum because he no longer trusted his voice.

What was he doing to her?

Sarah found if she moved her legs opposite from his, they swayed to the same rhythm, silent though it was. She closed her eyes. Instinct took over, giving her a sense of what to do. Her fingers stopped clutching and crept upward, seeking to anchor themselves around his strong neck. The stiffness went out of her spine and his hand spread over the small of her back, guiding her feet in better harmony with his. She turned her head and rested her cheek against his chest, and suddenly their movement together became natural, flowing freely from one step into the next.

So this was what it was to dance.

Sarah sighed and pressed closer, surrendering to the synchrony of two bodies moving as one. He cradled her head with his hand, intensifying her sense of oneness. From deep in her throat she could feel it, like a rising sound, and she began to hum a song she had never heard before, a song that matched the grace of the dance.

The moment lasted the length of her breath and sent her spirit soaring. She lifted her head to smile at him, and he chuckled when he saw her face.

"Move over, Fred and Ginger," he said.

"Who are Fred and Ginger?"

He laughed and tucked her head once again against his chest. "Can't you see them? Why, they're dancing right next to us. Ginger's got a floor-length gown on. It's kind of styled like your gray wool dress only it's pink and very frilly. And Fred is wearing a black coat with long tails and a ruffled white shirt and black pants with a shiny stripe down the side."

"A ruffled white shirt?" she asked, the words muffled. "On a man?"

"Oh, yes. He cuts a most dashing figure in it. Why don't you look for yourself?"

Zach loosened his hold and jerked his head sideways, indicating she should look behind him. His grin sent her tingling all the way to her toes.

She obeyed, taking in the rising slope of his chest muscles and the fine stretch of tendons underneath, and looked beyond his shoulder. Nothing was there but the blue walls cast in shadowy light and the windows, blank with the darkness of the night.

"Tell me what you see, Sarah," Zach said. "I need to hear you say that you believe in the magic of what's happening here."

His arms moved down to wreath her waist and draw her even closer. The swaying of their bodies began again and became more intimate, more concentrated at the place where she could feel the full heat and hardness of him. It added to her sense of confusion, her sense of total, irretrievable doom.

Dear Lord, she thought. Am I supposed to resist him now?

Gazing at him deepened her sense of standing at the edge of a great precipice. His eyes were heavy-lidded with desire and his jaw was clenched with the effort it took to control it, to hold her this way, and dance, and not rush. With a sense of great shock, she realized the Lord was not going to rescue her from this predicament. Zach would not be saved. And neither would she.

She felt dizzy. She shook her head to clear it, but the only reality was Zach, waiting for a sign. From Him or from her? she wondered, panicky. What had she expected? A burning bush outside the window? An angel charging in on a red horse? Such naiveté seemed ridiculous in the incredible clarity of this moment, and she wanted to laugh. Laugh, for God's sake.

Her body shook with hysterical relief. Relief that the struggle was over, that the devil in her had won. She could be herself now. Not a saint, she thought. Nor a sinner, either. Not with this man, a man she loved. And no longer a woman alone.

She opened her mouth to speak, but nothing came out. Zach must have sensed something significant was going on, however, for he stopped swaying and loosened his hold. "Sarah, I can't make you do this. You're shaking all over. I should have known this would happen . . . but I wanted you so much." He buried his face in her neck. "Forgive me."

"Shh, it's all right." She wreathed her arms around his neck and rubbed her cheek in the hollow of his chest.

"No, it's not," he said roughly. "It's wrong. You said so yourself. Wrong for you."

"How could it be wrong, this magic thing we're doing?" she murmured. She could feel his resistance and pressed a kiss at the base of his throat. "I want to be with you in this way, I truly do."

He went still. "I don't deserve this, Sarah," he whispered. "I was ready to take your virginity tonight, even though I knew it went against everything you believe in. How could you want to give such a gift to a man like me?"

"How could I not?" she answered, letting her tongue touch him. Whenever he did that to her, she always wanted to shiver.

He said her name on a sigh. "Sarah..."

She touched her tongue to him again, and lingered there, tasting him fully this time while she unbuttoned her blouse. Salt warm, he smelled of the good earth, rich and fervent. His hand came up to catch her hair. She could feel him winding it around his hand, and he tugged as though to test the strength of the bond.

"I need to know why you're doing this," he said, forcing her to look up at him by pulling her head back. But there was an unsteadiness to it that told her she was winning, and she answered by rocking her chin in a negative motion against his chest.

"No," she said. "You need to kiss me. Right here," she said, demonstrating on his chest where she wanted to be kissed. "And here," she said, edging her teeth around the flat disk of his nipple.

He inhaled sharply. His fingers, wound so thoroughly in her hair, gripped the back of her head. She did it again, using both her tongue and her teeth. He groaned and dragged his hand around to cradle her face.

"You'll regret this," he said hoarsely.

"No, I won't," she promised. The back of his hand grazed the curve of her cheek. "I won't," she repeated, and turned her head and kissed his fingers, too, and the top part of his chest as he loosened her hair, sending it in a wild cascade down her back. "I won't ever regret this."

He lifted her bodily, high enough that her face was above his, and looked up at her, his expression fierce. "Oh, yes,

ou will. I'm going to do exactly what you did to me. If it
eels half as good, it'll be torture, and you'll be begging me
o stop."

He set her on top of the tall bureau, knocking aside a vase
f flowers. They tumbled into her lap, spilling cold water
cross the front of her jeans. She gasped and he swore,
utting his hands on the splotches soaking her thighs. The
ressure was sudden, taking away the surprise, and her face
ust have showed it because he treated her to a wicked grin.
That was no accident. I wanted you wet."

His thumbs stroked her inner thighs, pushing her legs
part so he could lean against the front of the dresser. His
yes were level with her chin and he kissed her there, then
ower, making trails down her neck. She shivered. He took
mouthful of her open shirt between his teeth and tugged
away from her breast, exposing her nipple to the warmth
f his mouth.

His tongue followed, laving her openly, lovingly. She
asped in astonishment at the powerful sensations coursing
rough her and gripped his shoulders.

Zach breathed against her, imagining her gripping other
arts of his body. Her nipples responded to the hot flow of
ir, knotting into two pink points. Loving how she felt, how
e tasted, he used his lips to nuzzle the underside of one
reast while his hand came up to cup the other.

She whimpered and he grew more gentle, needing to know
what he was doing felt good to her. Her hand tightened
nd she arched more fully into his mouth. He suckled her
eeply then, going from one rosy crest to the other. He
ushed her blouse and bra from her shoulders, down her
rms. When her clothes finally fell to the floor, she buried
er hands in his hair.

His arms went around her. The skin above her waist band
elt like hot satin. The wooden barrier of the bureau against
e lower half of his body was painful, but he leaned into it
l the same and rubbed his chest against her bare breasts.

She angled closer and under the fingers he was using to stroke her spine, she became drawn like a bow, trembling with the severity of her need. He flattened his hand, giving her support. Meanwhile, the moisture left on her nipples burned its way through his skin. He became like flame, swaying to the rhythm they had discovered in the silence of the dance.

He drew back enough to unsnap his jeans and pull the zipper down. He was so rigid it hurt and he was suddenly afraid he would frighten her, so he didn't free himself. Instead he lifted her from the top of the wooden chest, holding the curve of her buttocks in the broadness of his hands. She curled her arms around his neck and her legs around his waist and he carried her that way to the bed, his mouth on hers, kissing her in the way he had kissed her breast, with the patience of a man who wanted to make sure his woman was good and ready for him.

With walking, his jeans eased past his hips. He laid her down with her head on a pillow, extracted a small foil package from his pocket, drew his jeans and his underwear off in the same motion, and levered his body to rest beside her. Her eyes widened when she saw the extent of his arousal. But when he would have turned and hitched his leg up to hide it, she faced him fully, and pressed her entire body flush against his.

It felt so good, he groaned and would have slid himself inside her right there, unable to help himself, if not for the denim barrier between her legs. Instead he continued the kiss he'd begun before, only this time, he wasn't very gentle. Invoking the rhythm of the dance, he plumbed her mouth to the beat, and she responded with a fierceness that shook his soul. He fumbled with the front of her jeans. She helped, her fingers as clumsy as his, and an eternity passed before he pushed the body-warm denim down her legs.

Her panties were made of slick nylon. He traced the brief band of material that covered her hip, knowing he had to go slow now. It was torture to pull back, but his reward was the look of her body in candlelight, completely bare except for the bit of ivory now beneath his hand.

Her skin glowed with the sheen of an exotic pearl. The dewy color was like something from a dream, cast in tones of gold, creating shadows that took on the texture of velvet. In profile, her nipples stood out like the tiniest rosebuds, tipped by the last lingering light of day, while the cleft between her breasts plunged into mystery, a mystery he had only begun to unravel.

He drank in the sight of her, aware of the fine thrumming of his body everywhere, especially the part that throbbed against her thigh. "You're so beautiful," he said.

"As are you." She laid her hand on his hip and mimicked what he was doing along the elastic of her briefs even though his skin was bare there. He swallowed, trying to hide his surprise that she would touch him so freely, and she lifted her hand and placed a finger at his Adam's apple. "Did that hurt you?" she whispered. "It feels so good when you touch me there, but maybe it is different for a man."

"It's no different," he said hoarsely. "I just wasn't expecting it."

"Why not?"

"Because you're new at this, Sarah. I thought, maybe, you'd be too shy."

"It's a little late for shyness, Zach. You have touched me everywhere. I want to do the same to you."

She stroked her hand down the middle of his chest and his heart thumped faster the lower she went. "I haven't touched you everywhere yet, Sarah," he said.

Her eyebrows drew together and her gaze touched his face. He slipped a finger beneath the elastic of her briefs and drew them down just a little, just enough to give her a clue as to what he meant.

Her hand slowed, drifting over his stomach. Then realization lit her features and she left off completely in amazement. Or so he thought.

"You mean . . ." she said on a husk. "You mean, I may touch you here, as well?"

Her finger stroked the most intimate part of his sex. He took a sharp breath, pulse leaping, skin jumping, and she pulled back as though stung, a sudden sheen in her eyes.

"I hurt you!"

"No, no, you didn't," he managed, catching her hand. He pressed it against his stomach, holding it there until she relaxed a little and he could properly use his vocal cords. "There is one major similarity between men and women that you should know about, though," he said.

"What's that?"

He let go of her and found the pressed line of her inner thighs. He stroked upward and dipped inside the rim of her panties, stroking the tightly curled hair he found there. "There are certain body parts which are very sensitive."

She pursed her lips on a rush of air. He soothed her with a kiss, letting his hand go slack against the soft triangle of cloth. Her mouth stayed surprised, opening under his, and he took advantage of it, suckling her with lips and tongue and teeth. She made a low sound and moved against the gentle weight of his hand.

He cupped her through the cloth. When it grew moist, he drew it down and she lifted her hips to help. Her fingers walked shyly down his belly, edging in the springy hair so like her own. He copied her caress and smiled a dare. She grew bolder, sliding her hand over his smooth, hot length. His fingers curved in ecstasy and probed her softest flesh, brushing it lightly until she tilted onto her back and arched in discovery. Her breath quickened and her legs closed, clenching around his hand. He could feel how tight she was, and he opened her very slowly with one finger, watching her face, letting her get used to him. Her face flushed with new color and her glazed eyes took on a feverish cast.

"Zach?" she whispered.

"Trust me, Sarah. Don't be afraid. Let it happen."

The heel of his hand rocked against her softness and he bent his head to her breast. Just grazing it was enough. She cried out and her release came suddenly, raining against his palm. Seeing her shudder caused a flash of heat to course through his body. He closed his eyes, feeling the edges of his control slip away. He took a deep breath and told himself he had to hold on for her. She deserved better than a rushed and desperate man.

He gathered her close. Tiny trembles shimmied down her arms. He chased them with his hands, rubbing her warm and ready for the final act of loving. She lifted her head and hugged him, the pressure of her body fierce. She rolled onto her back and he went with her, his flesh already probing hers. She spread herself open, begging him with her liquid doe eyes, nearly black in the guttering candlelight.

Sarah felt his penetration in tiny increments. He held himself rigid, poised above her, his restraint as awesome as the emotion in his eyes. They became her world and she lost herself in them, dissolving into a pile of loose limbs and supple bones. She never felt a lick of pain.

He filled her completely. A vibration went through her, low and deep, and the song she had made up for their dance came into her mind as he began to move within her.

This time the song didn't end with one lungful of air. This time it rose higher and higher, singing in her blood and the rhythm of two bodies becoming one. In the end, Zach broke it with the suspension of his final thrust. And when he finally came within her that one last time, the result was a moment of shared ecstasy and perfect flight, together in the arms of his beloved.

Ten

Zach woke with the sunrise. The poor light filtering in through the bedroom curtains made everything in the room look a variant of gray. Except Sarah.

He pulled the sheet down to his waist and propped his head on his hand so he could watch her sleep. She looked much younger with her eyes closed. Miniature fans of black lay against cheeks robbed of color, like marble in moonlight. Such contrast.

He picked up a loose tendril of long dark hair and arranged it on the pillow. He did it again with another loose curl, and another, until her hair fanned out like a black halo upon the dim percale. An angel, he thought. His angel.

She stirred, pushing at the coverlet as though she were too warm. He helped pull it down, and her hands came to rest, one flat against her bare stomach, the other in a loose fist under her chin. Shadows contoured her breasts and the curve of ribs underneath, softening the look of her rosy nipples, barely peaked. Because he could not resist, he lowered his head to kiss her there, gently, using only his lips because the prickle of his unshaven whiskers would wake her.

She tasted fuzzy warm, like the hazy light fanning across the bed, and he thought of the enormity of her sacrifice. He hadn't been able to appreciate it because he had been holding so firmly to all the things he wasn't willing to give up. Now his freedom seemed rather a petty thing, next to what she had given him.

He wanted to wake her, to say these words out loud that he couldn't say before. Love, he thought. My love. But there was one thing he wanted to give her while she slept, and that was to pay off his side of the bargain. He would go see the rest of the house.

He slipped out of bed and into his jeans. The floor was cold but he didn't want to take the time to put on his boots and socks. He left the door ajar and trod down the hall, hurrying, impatient now that the decision was made.

So little in the room of his childhood had changed. The only thing missing was the mass of posters that used to hang on the freshly painted blue walls. But his memory was not so easy to erase and he recalled the fights he used to have with his father about the swimsuit models and cars and rock-and-roll stars plastered ceiling-to-floor.

He walked around, touching the narrow bed, the chest of drawers, the spindly desk he swore had mocked him because he never used it. On the peg by the closet was a cowboy hat, black leather band on black brushed felt. "A chip off the old block," his father had said upon giving it to him on his seventeenth birthday.

Zach hadn't been able to disguise his horror. He'd left home for good less than a week later.

His hand went to the brim, and his finger skimmed the edge. He had never tried the hat on, never wanted to. The gift had come from his father, after all, accompanied by a cryptic message that told Zach he would always remain in another man's shadow, dancing to another man's tune. Swallowing, he lifted the hat from its peg and let the weight of it settle between his hands.

He could see his choices now; how Sarah had been right to insist on bringing him here. In rebelling against his father, he'd rebelled against everything remotely connected to the Bar M. Rather than stay and sort it all out, he'd chosen the freedom of transiency. It seemed the ultimate in liberation, but suddenly he saw how his thirst for adventure was still a thirst, one that hadn't been quenched in the Amazon or the Himalayas or anywhere else. And it wouldn't be, no matter where he went. He'd been so busy searching for the ultimate challenge, he hadn't realized what he already had.

The land, he thought. The land.

He went to the window and looked down on the garden below, a little microcosm of the Masterson ranch. It had sustained five generations, not in style, but in substance. He could see it now for what it was, unadorned and enduring, a setting for the pain in his life. But not the cause of it. Definitely not the cause of it.

In his youth, he had to blame someone, something. His mother, his father, the house in which he grew up. Now he knew better, knew that he, too, had made mistakes. He'd cut himself off deliberately, shoving everyone away out of fear. Sarah most of all. For she dared to save his life by offering him the kind of love he'd never had and always wanted.

How could he not love her? She was all that was good and pure and true. She gave unstintingly of herself, whatever the task. Yes, she was maddening, and stubborn, and had a mind of her own. And he loved her all the more for those things. It was a certainty now, in a way it hadn't been before when he'd suspected the motives of anyone or anything that went against his most cherished ideals. But wasn't that what love was? he mused. A reordering of priorities. A willingness to think beyond yourself, to give beyond your own capacity.

His hands tightened on the brushed felt hat brim. Zach went to the mirror and, very slowly, put the hat upon his head.

"You found it."

He whipped around. She was leaning against the frame of the door, wearing a navy flannel robe. Her glorious hair tumbled over one shoulder like a seal-brown waterfall streaked by sunshine. She clasped her hands and arrowed them up, holding them over her heart as though in prayer, and he saw the quiet pride in her eyes.

"It looks good on you."

Since he couldn't trust his voice, he acknowledged her with a flick to the brim, fighting his instinct to rip the hat off and pretend she hadn't witnessed a moment of profound importance. Instead he pivoted and studied the man in the mirror. "You think so?" he asked at last.

"I know so."

She came forward and halted in front of him, close enough to touch, the back of her head framed in the mirror by the broadness of his bronzed shoulder. Next to him, she looked so delicate and fragile. Yet, in many ways, she was stronger than he, stronger than he'd wanted to admit. He admitted it now by lifting his arm, though it trembled some, and beckoned her to stand beside him.

She fit herself along his body and looped her arms around his waist. Tilting her face up to smile at him, she said, "I think the color suits you particularly well."

"You don't think it makes me look like the bad guy in some Western movie?"

"Good men wear black hats, too. Does it fit all right?"

"Like it was made for me," he admitted, knowing it was. He kissed the top of her head and rubbed his cheek against her hair. "I've been awake for a while, poking around here. This used to be my room."

The pressure of her arms around his middle increased. "I figured as much. I found a number of calf-roping trophies with your name on them in the closet."

"From Little Britches Rodeos. I used to be pretty good."

"I'll wager you still are."

"It's a little like riding a bicycle. Some things you don't forget."

"Some things you're not supposed to forget."

"Didn't stop me from trying, though." He looked down at her and tried to smile, but he was crumbling inside. "Oh, Sarah," he said.

She led him to the bed and sat on the edge. He knelt on the floor in front of her, afraid in a way he'd never been before. The familiar and heady rush of adrenaline wasn't there. Instead he felt something gentler, something borne of hope rather than the threat of dying. He bowed his head and let Sarah's peaceful presence seep into him.

She took off the hat and laid it beside her on the striped green bedspread. Seeing the hat there, he recalled his father's hands on the brim, strong hands that were weather-worn and tracked with the scars of ten thousand days of stringing fence and baling hay. Strong hands that couldn't help but be helpless at times. Strong hands that were human.

Her arms came up to gather him close. He wept for the first time in many years, remembering the loneliness of his youth, needing to be held but being afraid of rejection, of losing all hope like his father had. And so he'd become somebody less than himself, rejecting everyone and everything of what he knew, and went off to carve his own place in the world. But some things weren't meant to be forgotten. And he'd denied his own soul for too long.

She held him that way a considerable time, murmuring quiet words of comfort. Her hands soothed the skin of his face and smoothed the hair at his brow. Eventually he let himself slip into the calm place she created and laid his head upon her lap.

When he had the strength, he asked the question that had been plaguing him these past five weeks. "How did you know I needed to come here?"

"I, too, have run away from the people and places I know best. When one has walked in the same moccasins, it is not a difficult thing to recognize."

He lifted his head and rocked back on his heels, wanting to see her face. "More pearls of wisdom from your father?"

"He was a wise man."

"I want to hear more about him."

"Yours first," she said. "He gave the hat to you, did he not?"

Zach nodded. "He could be stubborn as a mule and twice as hardheaded. Yet he had a soft spot in his heart for anything beautiful that came from nature. Snow in winter, rain in summer, the mountains and the plains. And animals. Especially animals. He used to let us kids keep a whole menagerie of them—horses, cats, dogs, whatever, even though the sheer numbers of what we had was hardly practical."

"You and he sound like you were cut from the same cloth."

Zach nodded, thinking of Sarah's love of the mountains. It had always touched him. As had her special relationship with Butcher, ornery cuss that he was. He pressed a kiss on her hand. "Dad would have liked you. You know what I remember most about him?"

"What?" she murmured, playing with his hair.

"The way he could sniff the wind and tell if a storm was coming, or look at a head of wheat to know exactly how much longer it needed to grow before it could be harvested, or ride herd on fifty head of cattle and sense instantly when one was missing. He had an awareness about him...a sense of...I don't know...it's hard to describe."

His voice trailed away and Sarah cupped his cheek. "A man of the land?"

He covered her hand and smiled. "A man of the land."

Sarah felt awe in watching Zach be reborn within his own skin. He was full of energy, full of plans. Over the next few days, he went to the new owners of the Bar M and offered to buy it back, eventually going so far as to make a bid twenty percent over the price the developer paid, the most Zach could afford. But the new owner said no. He had big plans of his own.

Fortunately, Zach was able to buy the house. The developer planned to dismantle it, anyway—he didn't mind charging Zach a few extra dollars to have it removed. So Sarah had an expert come out to assess the possibilities. The house was an excellent example of the architecture and building of its day, old enough to qualify as a historic building. It was also, essentially, a big square box. The expert planned to divide it in two, load it onto two flatbed semis and take it pretty much anywhere she and Zach wanted to go. Which meant they had to find a ranch of their very own to put it on.

Sarah knew she wanted to have a view of the mountains. And Zach wanted enough land to support a bona fide cattle operation. Even if he had been able to buy the Bar M back, his goal would not have been possible. Too many people now lived in the Boulder valley, and what was left of the Masterson's original land was not enough to subsist a rancher. So they decided they wanted a fairly big spread somewhere along the front range of the Rocky Mountains.

Easier said than done. Although Zach had a considerable amount of money saved from his travels, she had virtually nothing. His share of the proceeds from the sale of the Masterson ranch was not that large, either, not after being divided five ways between his siblings. They knew they were going to have to start small and work hard to upgrade and expand.

Zach confessed it was a scary thing for him to contemplate, living on the edge of disaster like that. He wanted to give her so much more. She reassured him, saying faith in the Lord above would carry them through no matter what happened. And Zach vowed to do whatever it took to make the new Bar M a success.

They spent a week charting their future in more ways than one, spending days reviewing ranch listings in Colorado and Wyoming, and nights reviewing the many ways of sharing love. By the time Sunday rolled around, they decided to hook the trailer up to the truck and spend the next three weeks together looking for their new spread.

Zach had driven into town Monday morning to pick up some last minute supplies before they left. Sarah heard the truck coming up the lane and ran to put on her coat. The day was clear and cold, with a gusty wind that could put the chill of the devil right through a body.

When she stepped outside she saw the truck wasn't the familiar white Ford Ranger that belonged to the ranch. This one was black, and relatively new, with a row of headlights attached to the hood of the cab. The windows were tinted, but she saw enough to spot a man's silhouette, wearing a baseball cap.

Ty came out of the bunkhouse and waved to her from across the yard. "You expecting someone?" he asked over the roar of the engine.

"No," Sarah called, shading her eyes against the glare reflected off the truck's shiny chrome. "You think it's the new owner?"

Ty shrugged and waited at the top of the bunkhouse steps. Butcher came running from his favorite hunting spot behind the main barn and skidded to a halt in the middle of the yard between Sarah and Ty, barking his fool head off.

The truck stopped in front of the bunkhouse, next to Ty's battered Chevy. The window rolled down and Ty sauntered down the steps to talk to the driver. Sarah saw a thick, sun-reddened neck and an outline of a broad shoulder covered in a plain shirt. The man gestured with a beefy hand, pointing at the barn, then the bunkhouse.

Hairs rose at the back of her neck. She froze, her breath short. But it couldn't be Cal. This man's jaw was clean-shaven. Besides, people of the Community didn't own trucks, didn't even know how to drive them.

Before her, Butcher stood his ground, still barking. He considered the entire ranch compound his territory now and let everybody know it, Ty and Zach included. Visitors got even worse treatment. Sarah stayed behind him, trying to catch a better glimpse of the man. He and Ty were having quite a conversation. Between barks, she heard snatches from Ty, but the other man's voice didn't carry.

Walking forward, she called Butcher and told him to hush. He whined and circled in front of her, lifting his nose to scent the air. Sarah noticed something else about the truck, something that made it different from other vehicles in these parts. The little rectangular plate in the back had Montana written on it.

The sick feeling grew in the pit of her stomach. Her steps quickened.

"Zach Masterson's the one you'll want to speak to about that. He should be home shortly if you'd like to wait," Ty said as she approached from behind. He touched the brim of his hat and stepped back, blocking her view, and nearly tripped over Butcher. The dog whimpered and went down on all fours, fawning at Ty's feet, his tail going a mile a minute.

"Hey, you old mutt," Ty said, bending forward to pet the dog. "You finally decided to make friends with me?"

"Ty, look out!" Sarah screamed.

She ran toward him, but it was too late. The truck door opened. She saw the familiar hobnailed boots hit the ground. Ty turned at the sound and the butt of the rifle hit him across the side of his head. He crumpled.

Sarah leapt and broke Ty's fall, but he was already unconscious. Choking back a sob, she clutched his limp body and staggered as she lowered him to the ground.

Above her came the sound of laughter. "Dumb cluck. Didn't you tell him I never give up, Sarah?"

She looked up to see Cal step away from the truck, the rifle held tight within his big fists. Butcher continued to fawn, cowering at his feet.

"No," she said. "You have no right."

Without taking his eyes from hers, he flipped the safety off the rifle. "I married your mother. That makes me your kin. The fifth commandment gives me the right."

"I will never honor you. My father is dead."

Cal lifted the rifle and aimed it at Ty's head. "Lessen you want the old man to end up like your pa, you'll change your tune mighty quick."

Zach drove into the yard and cursed. Ty Coburn's truck wasn't there, which meant he must have gone on an errand. Zach was hoping to get some help unloading the supplies he'd bought.

He spun the steering wheel with one hand and backed the truck as close to the trailer as he could get, for most everything needed to go in there. After Ty came back, they'd unload the supplies. Then, Zach told himself, he and Sarah could plan exactly when the two of them would leave to look for a ranch of their own.

Zach grabbed the mail and the bouquet of flowers wrapped in florist paper from the front seat and headed toward the house. The wind came up, ruffling the hair under his black cowboy hat. Zach didn't worry about it flying off. It fit that well.

Enjoying the feel of the cold, crisp air, he let the wind fill his coat. It was brand-new and he'd be needing it now that he'd made the decision to stay with Sarah and look for a place somewhere along the front range. Manuelo had accepted the decision with grace, especially when Zach gave up his share of their guide business in Brazil for the token sum of one dollar.

Clouds were rolling in from the north. He made a mental note to check the weather report for the next several days, for there was no point in leaving if he and Sarah were going to run into a major snowstorm. It was getting to be that time of year.

"Sarah?" he called when he stepped inside.

"In the kitchen," she answered from the back of the house.

She must be up to her elbows in something. Usually she came running out to meet him as though they'd been apart days or weeks rather than hours. Although he acted nonchalant about it, inside he was moved and always marveled at how freely she bestowed her affection. It made him feel like the luckiest man in the world.

"You know where Ty went off to?" He hung his coat on the hall tree, left his hat hanging on the banister at the bottom of the stairs, and picked up the mail and flowers. There were no more to be had in the garden, and whenever he'd gone into town this past week, he had brought her some fresh ones.

"No," she answered as he headed down the hall.

"Where's Butcher?" he asked as he stepped into the kitchen. "I didn't get the usual twenty-one-bark salute when I drove into the yard."

She stood at the sink piled high with suds, wearing her brown skirt and calico blouse. Her hair was pinned up in her old style, though lately she'd taken to wearing it down more and more. Especially if he offered to brush it for her.

"Out hunting, I suppose," she said.

He tossed his stuff onto the table and came up behind her, wrapping his arms around her waist while he nuzzled her shoulder. "You must be working hard. You're wearing your old clothes."

She ducked his kiss although her hand came out of the sudsy water and grabbed his wrist, holding on like she didn't want to let go.

"Where're your rubber gloves?" he asked. "That water is hot."

"It doesn't bother me," she said. "I'm used to it."

"I'm going to make sure our new place has a dishwasher. I don't like to see you working like a kitchen slave." He released her and stepped back to pick up the mail.

"I need to speak to you about that, Zach."

"I need to talk to you, too," he said, sorting through the mail. "While I was in town, I heard a good-size parcel of land is for sale in the Wind River area of Wyoming, south of the Grand Tetons. That's beautiful country, Sarah. I got a phone number and if the price is right, I think we should head there first when we leave tomorrow."

"That's what I wanted to talk to you about. I won't be going with you."

He stopped sorting and glanced at her. She had turned to face him, her hands wrapped in her long apron. For the first time, he noticed the gravity of her face and the faint shadows underlying her eyes. "Aren't you feeling well?"

"I'm fine."

"If we need to delay a few days because you're a little bit under the weather, that's okay, Sarah. Looks like there's a cold front moving through, anyway. And I got permission from the new owner to keep the house here until we've found a new place and we're ready to move it."

"It's not that at all," she said. "I've changed my mind about going."

"Sarah, you've got to come. I don't want to buy anything without your seeing it first. This is going to be our home, and I hope, our only one. I want us to pick it out together.''

"Zach, please. Don't make this more difficult for me than it already is.''

The way she avoided his eyes made his chest tighten. "What are you talking about?''

"I'm leaving.''

"Leaving?''

"I decided to wait and tell you to your face because I don't want you coming after me or trying to find me. That's all.'' She rushed past him and, out of some fog, he grabbed her arm.

"What did you say?''

She looked up at him, pleading with her eyes. "I can't do this,'' she whispered.

"Can't do what?'' he asked roughly, his grip tightening on her arm. What had she said? Had she actually told him she was *leaving?*

She gazed at the hand he had on her arm and her chin came up. "Let go of me,'' she said in a clear, cool voice.

"Not until you tell me what in hell is going on.''

Her eyes focused on a point somewhere past his shoulder, her expression remote and faraway. "I'm leaving you.''

The words hit him like a sledgehammer. "Why?'' he blurted, caught totally off guard. But the moment he asked the question, he knew he wasn't prepared to hear the answer. He loved her. And if she didn't love him, he wasn't sure how he would bear it. She meant that much to him now.

"I—''

"Wait,'' he interrupted. "Sit down.'' He pulled out a kitchen chair and plunked her down into it, none too gently, but his mind was working furiously, trying to think, casting about for something awful he may have said or done. Or not said or done. "I love you, Sarah. And I don't care if I have to marry you tomorrow to prove it, or drive around in a trailer with you to the ends of the earth or carry you upstairs and lock myself in a room with you for the rest of my life, but whatever this is, whatever has gotten to you, I know we can fix if we face it together."

She sat like a statue, unmoved. He lowered himself into the chair next to hers and took her limp hand, fear sending his heart racing. Steeling himself for whatever might come next, he forced her to look at him. "Tell me why, Sarah."

"I don't want to be with you anymore."

He wouldn't have believed her if her voice had been as dull and listless as her hand. But it was alive with feeling and her eyes glittered with a passion he'd come to associate with their lovemaking. Something essential withered inside him. He wondered for a split second if he'd entirely misjudged her from the very beginning. "You don't know what you're saying."

"Yes, I do. I know exactly what I'm saying. I'm saying goodbye. And I don't want you to think about me ever again."

He felt the sting of tears at the back of his throat. "Sarah, don't do this to us."

"There is no us, Zach."

"No us? No us!" He jumped up and raked his hands through his hair. "What have we been doing in that bedroom upstairs for the past week if there is no us?"

"It was a dream. A foolish dream."

He lifted her bodily, hands on her upper arms. "Not a dream, Sarah. And not foolish, either. What exists between us is the most real thing I have ever experienced. And I *know* it's the same for you. You couldn't respond to me in the way that you do unless you felt it, too. Oh, I know we haven't had much chance to tell each other how much we care—no, *love,* one another—but that doesn't mean it's not real. Love is more than words. It's thought and feeling and action and . . ."

He jerked her to him and kissed her, unable to think of what else to do. He could offer no better proof. After her first moment of shock when her lips parted instinctively with his, she pummeled him with her fists and cried, ''No, no, no. You're wrong. Please, just go away and leave me alone.''

She wrenched away and covered her face, crying as if her heart were about to break. Zach had never really seen her cry before. It scared him like nothing else ever had. He didn't understand her. Lord knew, he probably never would, but he could see her distress and knew that he, somehow, was the cause. Whatever this thing was, he couldn't fix, and he'd never felt so helpless in his life.

He kicked a chair out of the way, sending it crashing into the wall. She jumped and backed up, her eyes going from the door to him and back again. She obviously wanted him to go. She had practically screamed at him to go. And he was suddenly afraid he would physically hurt her if he didn't go. Right now.

He banged his way outside, so frustrated and angry he couldn't see straight. He didn't have his coat or his hat and the cold ran through him like an ice storm, freezing him to the bone. Or had Sarah done that?

Yes, Sarah, had done that.

He took the four stairs off the back porch in one leap and strode past the garden, his boot heels ramming the hard ground with every step. He wanted to hit something. Instead he jammed his fists into his pockets and reached deep for a reason, for a thought that made sense. But his stomach churned and his muscles shook with the effort it took to contain himself. This can't be happening. How could she want to leave?

He entered the orchard, blinded by the cold and the brightness of the sun. And tears. Tree trunks caught his shoulders, his elbows, and finally, an exposed root tripped him. He went sprawling. Frost-edged leaves cushioned the fall. He pushed himself up and got his legs underneath him, but his breath fogged the air and he felt as if his lungs would burst if he took another step. He was dying, dying, and all because of her.

He caught himself against a tree, remembering the time he had pinned her to one and treated her so brutally. Maybe that's why she wanted to leave. Even with all the ghosts he had faced in the past few weeks, he still wasn't good enough. He was still capable of brutality. Look what he had done to that chair inside.

The truth was, he would never be good enough for her. Just like he had never been good enough for his father or his mother or anyone else in his life. Only with Sarah had he felt a faint ray of hope that maybe, just maybe, he could be loved just for himself. He had never met anyone like her. She gave herself completely, holding nothing back. A truer, purer soul never existed. And she never lied, which was why hearing her say she didn't want to be with him anymore was like having acid poured in his ears. Sarah didn't hurt people out of malice or spite. Hell, she'd give her own life to save someone else if it came right down to it.

Zach leaned his forehead against the tree trunk. Rough bark bit his skin. He welcomed the pain because it was better than confronting what he felt inside. The wind picked up, whistling through the bare branches, echoing the words in his head.

She would give her own life.

Give her own life.

Her life.

He went very still.

Turning, he faced the house. It looked picture perfect—the contrast between white clapboards and black shutters vivid and strong. Everything was so neat—the garden, the fence, the empty laundry poles. But Zach knew from experience it had looked that way before. And looks could be deceiving.

He ran.

Eleven

Zach's worst fears were realized. Halfway back to the house, he heard a gunshot. It came from outside the house, somewhere in front. He pounded past the garden, cut through the windbreak of cottonwoods between house and barn, and spotted Sarah being dragged to the trailer by a large man. The flare of her skirt was the last thing he saw before the door slammed.

He dashed across the yard, leapt the two wooden steps leading up to the door and barreled through.

They were all there in the tiny trailer—Sarah, Coburn, Butcher...and Cal. The strange man holding the rifle on Sarah had to be him. Held up by suspenders, his pants were made from the same brown material as her skirt, and a simple homespun shirt pulled across the meaty muscles of his chest. Butcher stood rigid at his side, as though an invisible leash went from the dog's neck to the man's thick wrist. Apparently the months with Sarah hadn't erased Cal's control over Butcher.

"Don't move, or I'll blow him away," Cal said.

Zach registered the firepower of the semiautomatic Remington 742 now pointed at Coburn's head. The old ranch hand was bound and gagged, with chains wrapped around his hands and feet. He sat slumped over in a chair pulled up beside the bed, obviously unconscious. His temple was misshapen and bruised a sickly yellow. Dried blood was visible in the weathered lines of his neck.

Zach put up his hands, nice and easy. "Okay," he said. "I'm not going anywhere."

His gaze went to Sarah. She stood on the other side of the bed, opposite Coburn, her hands clasped tightly in front of her, her wrists bound by a length of rope, the shaking of her head nearly imperceptible. He could tell how sorry she was for the things she had been forced to say to him. Two high spots of color banded her cheeks and her eyes were bright with unshed tears.

Cal aimed the rifle at Zach. "We tried to get rid of you but you just didn't want to walk away, did you? Now you get to join our little party. Sit."

Knowing he'd have to move fast when the opportunity came, Zach perched on the side of the bed closest to Coburn. His years in the jungle had taught him how to make a weapon out of anything and the trailer was loaded with possibilities. In the tiny adjoining kitchen, there were knives in the drawers and glasses in the cabinets. His mind rattled off the choices in rapid succession. There was Coburn's chair and the chest of drawers. He'd even use the damn bed if he had to. And if he could get hold of that mean-looking chain coiled in front of Sarah, it would make a helluva takedown device, thank you very much. The key was distraction, and keeping Sarah and Coburn safe.

Cal glanced at Sarah and jerked his head toward Zach. "Tie him up," he said.

Sarah reached for the chain. Cal had left about a foot of rope between her wrists, giving her room to use her hands but not her arms. As she came toward him, Zach noticed she moved stiffly, as though walking were painful. He glanced down and saw another length of rope tied around her ankles. She also wore thick wooden clogs on her feet.

"Don't try anything, either of you," warned Cal.

Zach held out his hands and watched Sarah loop the middle of the chain around his wrists. Her fingers were like ice. He kept his gaze averted from her face but moved his leg against her skirt, slightly pressuring her to move sideways. She knelt in front of him, the nod of her head subtle in the downward tilt of her head, and pulled the chain down from his wrists to his ankles.

Zach made his move. He exploded off the bed, pushing Sarah behind him while hooking the leg of Coburn's chair. It toppled backward, out of harm's way.

The rifle went off. Zach feinted left and swung his arms together straight up and over his head. The chain whistled through the air. Cal threw up an arm to block it, and the rifle tipped toward the floor.

Zach charged, bowling Cal over. The chain tangled around his wrists as they grappled on the floor, and Zach knew from the weak shakiness in his arms he'd been shot. "Run, Sarah, run!" he yelled.

"Butcher!" Cal commanded. "Attack!"

The dog landed on Zach's back, snapping and snarling.

"Butcher, no!" Sarah screamed.

Zach felt the dog being jerked off his back. Knowing Sarah had done it, he made one last-ditch effort and wrenched at the rifle. It skittered across the floor, out of reach.

Cal bellowed his rage, sending Butcher into a frenzy of barking. Sarah screamed again and Zach managed to duck the punch Cal aimed at his face. It landed on his shoulder, sending him rolling left. Cal staggered up, pivoted and kicked him square in the ribs. Pain exploded through his gut.

Clutching his side with one hand, Zach lunged desperately for the gun with the other, but Cal reached down and scooped it up.

"No!" Sarah let go of Butcher and rushed toward Cal. He quickly brought the rifle to bear, forcing her to stop short, teetering in the clumsy clogs.

Cal turned the gun on Zach. "Lover boy's a dead man now."

"No! Please!"

Zach curled his body around the searing pain along his left side. His breath came out in labored heaves. The maniac had not only shot him, he'd cracked some of his ribs, as well. "Sarah, save yourself," he rasped. "Don't worry about me."

Sarah hobbled to him. Cal intercepted, hooked one arm around her neck and forced her spine up against his chest, dragging her backward. She faced outward, eyes huge and fearful. "I won't kill him, Sarah. I'll let Butcher do it."

"No!"

Zach watched helplessly as Sarah raised her bound hands and pushed at Cal's meaty arm struggling to keep the pressure off her throat. But her strength was no match for the man. Butcher barked excitedly from the door of the trailer, ears pricked.

"Come here, boy," Cal called.

"No, Butcher," Sarah gasped. "Stay."

The dog circled in place, obviously confused. Cal shoved Sarah away from him into the opposite corner and said with authority, "Come, Butcher."

"Stay," Sarah ordered, her voice tremulous.

Butcher whined and cocked his head, his brown eyes going from Cal to Sarah.

"Butcher," Cal warned, and shook his gun slightly. "Come."

Butcher immediately bounded forward.

"Stay!"

Butcher hunkered down on his belly and looked at Sarah, his tail wagging. He crept sideways toward Cal.

"That's right, boy. Come on." Cal took a step forward, rattling the gun.

"Butcher, no," Sarah said, her voice drowned by the rattling. She rushed by Cal, trying to reach the dog first.

Cal stuck out his foot and tripped her. She fell, yet managed to remain upright by catching a corner of the bed. Zach gritted his teeth and reached out to steady her, his hand smeared with blood.

Feeling Zach's support, Sarah straightened. Cal laughed and gave Butcher a quick pat, then motioned the dog back over to stand guard by the door. Crossing the room in two strides, Cal poked the barrel of the rifle into Zach's belly.

Sarah clasped her hands together in eloquent entreaty. "Don't hurt him anymore, Cal. Please."

Chuckling, Cal shoved the rifle in harder. Zach grunted in pain. "Ain't nothing better than a bullet to the gut to torture a man, Sarah. Did you know that?"

"Please," Sarah pleaded. "Stop it."

"Doesn't kill him right away, you see. Oh, no. Just tears right through the intestines. Even today, modern medicine can't always control the resulting infection. It's a slow death. Nice and slow."

The barrel dug deeper. Zach closed his eyes with the effort it took not to scream.

"Cal, don't," Sarah begged, feeling tears run down her face. "I'll do anything."

"Anything?" Cal asked, his motion arrested.

"Don't, Sarah," Zach rasped.

Cal rammed the rifle in harder. "You shut up, lover boy."

Sarah dropped to her knees. "Cal, I beg you. I'll do anything you say, even go with you. Only please don't hurt him."

"Sarah, no," Zach croaked.

"Oh, yes," Cal said. "A mighty interesting proposal. Let me think on it a minute."

He let the barrel of the rifle wander in Sarah's direction. Zach bit his lip until it bled, vowing not to make a sound.

"I'll go with you back to the Community," Sarah said. "It will be just like before."

"Not exactly like before," answered Cal. "Before you were my stepdaughter. Now I want you as my wife. And we wouldn't be able to return to the Community," Cal continued. "When you ran away, the Elders found that flashlight, and discovered that I was doing other forbidden things, like using the truck to expand access to my cattle herds. So I've been banished. Which means if you agree to come with me, you'll have to say goodbye to everyone and everything you've ever known." The rifle swung toward Zach. "Including lover boy here."

Sarah nodded. "If you don't hurt Zach and Ty any more, then, yes, I'll do whatever you want."

"No, Sarah," implored Zach.

"Swear on God's Word," said Cal.

"Don't, baby," whispered Zach. He hitched himself up on one elbow. If he could get close enough to Cal, maybe he could sweep him off his feet from behind...

"You stop moving and shut your trap!" Cal roared, and grabbed Sarah's arm, hauling her to her feet. "Or I'll strip her and take her right here!"

It wrenched Zach to the bottom of his soul to watch Sarah swear on all that was holy to submit unto Cal in all ways. He closed his eyes, using every ounce of strength he had to drag himself forward.

"Now tell lover boy goodbye, Sarah, for you'll never see him again in your life."

Zach opened his eyes to find her kneeling next to him. With her help, he made it to his knees and he clung to her, his senses reeling. He couldn't even see straight. How could he save her? He cupped her cheek and brought her near so she could hear his broken whisper. "Baby, you can't do this You can't go with him. He'll kill you."

She shook her head. "I love you. I'll always love only you—"

"Don't say that to him!" screamed Cal. "You belong to me! Only me!"

Cal slammed the butt of the rifle into the wall above Sarah's head. "Tell him you don't love him! Tell him that I'm going to take his place!"

Sarah threw herself over Zach, protecting him from the rain of plaster spilling from the wall. Zach gripped her, too his arms trembling across her back. Then he slumped against the wall, barely conscious. "Sarah..."

The rain stopped as abruptly as it had begun. Cal backed up and aimed the rifle at Sarah. "Get away from him."

Sarah slowly withdrew from Zach's embrace, not knowing how else to protect him. Butcher whined and his nails clicked on the trailer floor.

"Stay, you damn dog," Cal muttered.

Sarah wanted to look, to see where Butcher was, but the black barrel of the rifle was only inches from her face.

"Now, you look directly into lover boy's eyes and you tell him you don't love him."

Sarah didn't move.

"Tell him!"

She shook her head mutely. Zach cracked open his eyes found her hand and squeezed. "Tell me, Sarah," he whispered. "He'll kill you if you don't."

"That's right," Cal echoed. "I'll kill you if you don't."

"No," she whispered.

Zach tightened his grip. "We know what's real, don't we Sarah? You can tell me. I won't mind."

Sarah stared at his dear and ravaged face, and knew that she would give her own life rather than betray her feelings for Zach. "You are my one true love, Zach. And, no matter what happens, I will love you to Heaven and beyond."

Sarah shrieked as she was jerked to her feet. Zach used everything he had and swung his legs to trip Cal up, but he brushed the feeble kick off as though it were a fly, and hauled Sarah across the room by the hair.

"I'll kill you myself if you hurt her!" Zach yelled. With superhuman effort, he used his right arm to somehow prop himself higher. Blood bubbled up his throat.

Cal threw Sarah onto the bed and jumped on top of her. She screamed. Coughing, Zach used the wall to climb to a standing position.

The room tilted, reeled. Zach staggered toward the bed. Beyond the roaring inside his head, he heard a terrible snarling. Out of a red mist, he saw Butcher hurl himself at Cal. There was a scream and the sound of ripping flesh.

Cal fell to the floor, eyes bulging, hands at his bloodied throat.

Zach fell across the bed and gathered a sobbing Sarah against his heart. She was safe.

The terror was over.

Epilogue

Sarah stood at the window of the master bedroom and looked down at the front yard below. It lay shadowed in the dim time between moonset and sunrise, when the clouds to the east were showing the first faint streaks of dawn. A lantern bobbed in the semidarkness, carried by a man wearing a long sheepskin duster. Ty Coburn, right on schedule.

Sarah smiled. Although the silver-haired man often professed his undying devotion to the Masterson ranch because of her cooking, she'd had to promise to make his favorite shoofly pie for dessert tonight before he would agree to prepare breakfast for the ranch hands this morning. Ever since their run-in with Cal, Ty had been taking considerable advantage of her expertise with shoofly pie.

Sarah turned from the window and glanced at the four-poster behind her. Zach lay on his back, sprawled across the rumpled sheet and blankets, asleep. He'd pulled on blue jeans when he'd gotten up to bring little Matthew in for the

3:00 a.m. feeding, but except for the flannel-wrapped baby bundle, anchored by a large brown hand, his chest was bare.

She drifted over and perched on the edge of the mattress, loosening her robe against the heat of the room. With the baby's arrival coinciding with the chill of autumn, Zach had insisted on keeping the modern gas furnace in the basement blasting most of the time.

Exhaustion stamped his features. She really should let him rest. Between the harvest just completed and the birth of his son, he'd been running short on sleep for many weeks. But she had planned this morning carefully for a reason, and since she'd arranged for one of the other ranch hands to do Zach's chores this morning, he could sleep later, when Matthew woke again to be fed.

She slid her hands beneath the blue bundle and lifted, careful of the tiny head covered in soft black down. Kissing the tiny fragile spot on top, she carried him to his own room just down the hall. If she were lucky, he'd give her an hour before he wakened for the day.

By the time she returned, Zach had rolled over onto his side, his back to her. She took off her robe and crawled naked into bed next to him. Her feet were freezing. She snuggled close and wrapped her arms around him, letting his sleep heat warm her. Beneath her elbow, the long puckered scar on his left side reminded her of that horrible day when Cal had come to take her away.

After Butcher had attacked and killed him, she'd dissolved into a fit of hysterical weeping. Zach had crawled over and tried to comfort her, but the bullet wound on his left side had bled profusely. He'd collapsed.

She'd known enough to run to the bunkhouse and call 911. When the ambulance had finally screamed into the yard, it was the first time she had ever seen one up close, but she'd felt only relief, and a panicky fear. The extent of Zach's and Ty's injuries had gone well beyond her ability to treat with simple first aid and herbal remedies.

The police had been called when Cal's body was discovered, and Butcher had been remanded and taken to the animal control pound. It was only after an extended investigation and a demonstration by Sarah of how well he'd been trained, that the coroner's office issued a statement of accidental death. Then the animal control office agreed to turn Butcher over to Sarah's custody on the condition that he no longer be allowed to live in Boulder County. Since they were moving, anyway, Sarah had been only too eager to comply.

Zach had insisted on marrying immediately, in front of a judge in the hospital where he and Ty Coburn had been recovering. A groggy Ty, in consideration of his concussion and the white bandage that wound around his head, had sat in a wheelchair during the ceremony, serving as best man. Betsy Miller, Jason Miller's wife, who happened to be a nurse at the hospital and a frequent visitor, had served as Sarah's attendant.

Sarah had worn a simple white dress she'd bought by herself at Amsterdam's. When Zach had noticed that it still carried price tags, he'd smiled and cut them off himself. He'd worn blue jeans and his boots and not much else, for his ribs were taped and the wound in his side still draining.

They'd had another ceremony one month later, before God, at the start of the new year, in the snowswept yard of their new home in the Wind River Valley. Traveling to witness it were Zach's brother, Bram, and his beautiful wife, Mandy, and last but not least, Joe and Elizabeth and Meg. Mastersons all, they'd stood, irreverently grinning, while Sarah and Zach had taken the most traditional of vows.

He claimed there was no feeling around the scar because the nerves had been severed and would take years to grow back. Warm now, Sarah kissed him there first and traced the healed line with her tongue. She checked his face, the lean brown of his cheeks, the network of tiny lines relaxed in sleep, the strong marks of past grins bracketing his mouth,

nd felt such a strong feeling of love she pushed him onto his
ack and straddled him. She laid the top half of her body
own on top of his chest and let herself fall into the feeling,
llowing it to lodge itself deep and send tiny throbs of hap-
iness singing through her veins. Here was where she be-
onged, she thought.

"What are you doing to me, woman?" Zach asked, his
voice slumberous and hoarse.

"What do you think I'm doing?" she asked, and ran her
and down his long arms, firm strokes this time, designed
o bring him into full wakefulness. He stirred and a crease
ppeared between his brows. She hitched herself up and
issed him there, and then his mouth, parted in half sleep
ut soon carnal and open beneath hers. His hands spread
pon the small of her back and she shifted slightly to rub
erself against his sex, already so full and hard between her
egs.

"Am I dreaming?" he asked into her mouth. "It's been
o long."

"Three months," she murmured, thinking of the last six
weeks of her pregnancy and the six weeks of recovery
ince—long weeks of holding and loving each other with
ands and mouths but little else.

"How could I give this up for three months? I must be
reaming."

She opened wider in answer, feeling how the blood
ounded in her ears, and she thought of the life that had so
ecently grown to fruition inside her, the life Zach had
tarted on their first night of marriage before God. She felt
uch need quickening inside her, ripe and ready, beckon-
ng, pulling. She was glad of the precautions she'd taken,
his gift she had given her husband, the gift of protection
nd planning and time for him and for herself. There would
e more children, but they would be given life as a loving
God wished, when she and Zach were ready.

"Are you sure, Sarah? It seems so soon. And you've been so tired, having to get up with the baby and all."

"You, too," she chided.

"Yeah, well, I get to sleep during feeding time."

His palms pressed her distended nipples, desensitized by their new role. A tingling went from the centers out, making her realize little Matthew hadn't quite sucked her dry. "Yes," she said, "I'm very sure. I want to feel you inside me."

"Lord, I want that, too. But I'm not prepared for this, honey. I mean, we talked about waiting awhile before we try for more kids, but we didn't really discuss who's responsible for the birth control."

"Shh," said Sarah. "You don't have to worry. The county nurse visited yesterday."

"I thought she came to give Matt his vaccinations."

"She also came to examine me, and pronounced me fit as a fiddle."

"You're fit, all right," Zach groaned. "And so tight. I wish I could fit into you right now."

"Please do," she said, positioning herself so he was poised at her entrance.

Zach groaned. The contractions of her opening were so powerful he could feel himself being drawn in. He grabbed her and held her still in an agony of suspended longing. "Sarah, we talked about this. I need to use a condom until we're ready to have more children."

"There is no need for a condom, Zach."

She rocked against him and sheathed just the tip of his sex. The feeling was so exquisite, he knew he would risk it. Then he remembered how he had vowed to cherish this woman all the days of his life. He wouldn't allow her to be wrung out by too much work and too many children in too short a time. He started to withdraw, but she reached down and guided him fully inside her. He nearly passed out with the pleasure of it.

"The nurse gave me something special so we could do this without fear. A little rubber cap..."

He didn't hear the rest because he was drowning in sensation. The feel of her body covering his, not only with her weight but with her generosity, as well, touched him like nothing else could. Her willingness to adapt her beliefs inspired him to do the same, to find God in his own heart.

He took her hair and wrapped it around his hands, feeling the silken texture, the way it bound him to her. And he was glad. He let her hair spill around their heads, a curtain of privacy that created a space where serenity lived. He gentled his kiss in spite of his burning desire to bury himself in her. Sarah liked gentleness.

She sighed and sank onto him. He felt a quaking take his heart, a biological echo of his soul, so moved by the trust she placed in him, the purity he found in this specialness they created. He held her hips, drawing the dance out, listening to her breathe, then pant, the slickness building between them. Finally he felt her tighten at intervals, the soaring begun.

He clutched her then, thrusting deep and fast. And they went there together, forged in body and spirit, to the place where heart, mind and soul come together.

Home.

*   *   *   *   *

Get Ready to be Swept Away by
Silhouette's Spring Collection

Abduction
& Seduction

These passion-filled stories explore both the dangerous
desires of men and the seductive powers of women.
Written by three of our most celebrated authors, they are
sure to capture your hearts.

Diana Palmer
Brings us a spin-off of her Long, Tall Texans series

Joan Johnston
Crafts a beguiling Western romance

Rebecca Brandewyne
New York Times bestselling author
makes a smashing contemporary debut

Available in March at your favorite retail outlet.

MILLION DOLLAR SWEEPSTAKES (III)

No purchase necessary. To enter, follow the directions published. Method of entry may vary. For eligibility, entries must be received no later than March 31, 1996. No liability is assumed for printing errors, lost, late or misdirected entries. Odds of winning are determined by the number of eligible entries distributed and received. Prizewinners will be determined no later than June 30, 1996.

Sweepstakes open to residents of the U.S. (except Puerto Rico), Canada, Europe and Taiwan who are 18 years of age or older. All applicable laws and regulations apply. Sweepstakes offer void wherever prohibited by law. Values of all prizes are in U.S. currency. This sweepstakes is presented by Torstar Corp., its subsidiaries and affiliates, in conjunction with book, merchandise and/or product offerings. For a copy of the Official Rules send a self-addressed, stamped envelope (WA residents need not affix return postage) to: MILLION DOLLAR SWEEPSTAKES (III) Rules, P.O. Box 4573, Blair, NE 68009, USA.

EXTRA BONUS PRIZE DRAWING

No purchase necessary. The Extra Bonus Prize will be awarded in a random drawing to be conducted no later than 5/30/96 from among all entries received. To qualify, entries must be received by 3/31/96 and comply with published directions. Drawing open to residents of the U.S. (except Puerto Rico), Canada, Europe and Taiwan who are 18 years of age or older. All applicable laws and regulations apply; offer void wherever prohibited by law. Odds of winning are dependent upon number of eligible entries received. Prize is valued in U.S. currency. The offer is presented by Torstar Corp., its subsidiaries and affiliates in conjunction with book, merchandise and/or product offering. For a copy of the Official Rules governing this sweepstakes, send a self-addressed, stamped envelope (WA residents need not affix return postage) to: Extra Bonus Prize Drawing Rules, P.O. Box 4590, Blair, NE 68009, USA.

SWP-S295

is

DIANA PALMER'S
THAT BURKE MAN

He's rugged, lean and determined. He's a
Long, Tall Texan. His name is Burke, and he's
March's *Man of the Month*—Silhouette Desire's
75th!

Meet this sexy cowboy in Diana Palmer's
THAT BURKE MAN, available in March 1995!

Man of the Month...only from Silhouette Desire!

DP75MOM

A new series from Nancy Martin

Who says opposites don't attract?

Three sexy bachelors
should've seen trouble coming
when each meets a woman
who makes his blood boil—
and not just because she's beautiful....

In March—
THE PAUPER AND THE PREGNANT PRINCESS (#916)

In May—
THE COP AND THE CHORUS GIRL (#927)

In September—
THE COWBOY AND THE CALENDAR GIRL

Watch the sparks fly as these handsome hunks fall for
the women they swore they didn't want!
Only from Silhouette Desire.

Robert...Luke...Noah
Three proud, strong brothers who live—and
love—by

THE CODE OF THE WEST

Meet the Tanner man, starting with
Silhouette Desire's *Man of the Month* for
February, Robert Tanner, in Anne McAllister's

COWBOYS DON'T CRY

Robert Tanner never let any woman get close
to him—especially not Maggie MacLeod. But
the tempting new owner of his ranch was
determined to get past the well-built defenses
around his heart....

And be sure to watch for brothers Luke and Noah,
in their own stories, COWBOYS DON'T QUIT
and COWBOYS DON'T STAY, throughout 1995!

Only from

SILHOUETTE®
Desire®
Hearts of Stone

Three strong-willed Texas siblings whose rock-hard
protective walls are about to come tumblin' down!

A new Silhouette Desire miniseries by

BARBARA McCAULEY

March 1995

TEXAS HEAT (Silhouette Desire #917)
Rugged rancher Jake Stone had just found out that he
had a long-lost half sister—and he was determined to
get to know her. Problem was, her legal guardian and
aunt, sultry Savannah Roberts, was intent on keeping
him at arm's length.

August 1995

TEXAS TEMPTATION (Silhouette Desire #948)
Jared Stone had lived with a desperate guilt. Now he
had a shot to make everything right again—until the
one woman he couldn't have became the only woman
he wanted.

Winter 1995

TEXAS PRIDE
Raised with a couple of overprotective brothers,
Jessica Stone *hated* to be told what to do. So when
her sexy new foreman started trying to run her life,
Jessica's pride said she had to put a stop to it. But her
heart said something *entirely* different....